By Accident

By Accident

SUSAN KELLY

PEGASUS BOOKS
NEW YORK

BY ACCIDENT

Pegasus Books LLC
80 Broad Street, 5th Floor
New York, NY 10004

First Pegasus Books edition 2010

Interior design by Maria Fernandez

Library of Congress Cataloging-in-Publication Data is available.

ISBN: 978-1-60598-088-1

10 9 8 7 6 5 4 3 2 1

Printed in the United States of America
Distributed by W. W. Norton & Company

In memory of my father,
Freddy Stafford

By Accident

Chapter One

I OPENED THE DOOR TO WHIT'S BEDROOM, PASSED THE hump in the bed, pulled the slatted blinds open, and looked out at our poplar tree, whose leaves this March of his spring break were no larger than ears. The view from Whit's second-story window was the same as from Russ's and mine: a dozen smallish houses, four brick, six clapboard, all one-storied—across and down Liberty Ave. "I booked us at the Omni for graduation weekend."

Beneath the quilt, Whit's voice was muffled. "Don't do it, Mom."

"Why not?"

"You'll jinx me, making reservations three months ahead of time. I'll get expelled or flunk or won't get into college. Wait until May." The heap in the bed elongated as he stretched to full height, and the footboard creaked from the pressure of his toes. "What's that?"

I listened. "Sounds like the theme from *Mulan*."

Whit's curly brown hair emerged from the same red-white-and-blue zig-zagged patterned sheets that I'd taken to boarding school and never discarded; linens grown soft and faded and dated from years of launderings. "When did Disney music get so *sad*?" he asked, then wrapped his arm around the pillow and inclined his head toward his bicep, silently saying *Watch this* as he flexed, forming a muscled bulge. He laughed at his own vanity. "Does Ebie have to practice the piano now, on a Saturday?"

"She's playing, not practicing, and it's also one in the afternoon."

The fourteen-hour nights—and days—her teenagers spent sleeping annoyed my friend Anne, who was married to Russ's partner in Lucas Contractors. "Why?" I'd asked her. "If they're not awake they're not asking for the car or watching television or leaving the kitchen in shambles or tying up the telephone."

"I don't know why," Anne had stubbornly insisted. "It's just *wrong*."

Anne was five years older than I, and the same span separated our children, so she'd been my standard over the years for weekly allowances, television time, punishments, even when we got a dog. "The McCalls got their dog when Dixon was eleven," I'd told Whit when he began begging in first grade.

"You can wait until then, when you're old enough to handle the responsibility of looking after a pet."

Ebie thudded upstairs and leapt on Whit. She mashed her palm to the crushed, cherubic ringlets her brother had hated throughout childhood but appreciated now for their wash-and-wear ease. "The college chicks are going to love my hair, Mom," he'd told me.

"You have bed head," Ebie informed him.

"And you're going down, Miss Elizabeth," he growled, then grabbed her, pulling her under the covers with him, trashing the bedclothes.

I thought of Anne's rolled-eyed observation: "A teenage male always has to be *touching* someone. Preferably someone soft and female."

"Careful how you wrestle with Ebie," I'd cautioned Whit.

"Why?"

"Because it hurts."

"I don't hurt her."

I'd put the carrot peeler on the counter, turned to face him, and gestured to my breasts. "Here."

"Mom!" he managed to protest despite a flush of embarrassment. "She doesn't have anything *there*."

"How do you know? When you were ten, did it hurt if someone accidentally hit you in—"

"Okay, okay," he'd conceded.

"Better bed head than pea head," I said now. In

some barbaric boarding school ritual of solidarity and machismo, Whit had shaved his head with the rest of the Windsor School lacrosse team. He'd sat down in the barber's chair, said, "I'll have a number four," and stood up bald. I looked out the window again. "This time last year he was hairless, and I have pictures to prove it."

Putting her hand on my shoulder for balance, Ebie scrambled to her knees on the folding chair, one of several hundred arranged on the grass for the out-door ceremony. Tightly furled vanilla diplomas stood sentry in a mahogany box on the dais. "Where's Whit?" she asked.

I craned to see through the milling crowd of families and guests claiming the seats saved earlier with programs and handbags, even masking tape. Through pastel linen shifts and flowy flowery skirts, through shy sisters and lanky-limbed brothers and striped seersucker suits, around the occasional hat and bow-tied neck. They were gathering in the deep pool of blue shade near Turner Hall, a crowd of eighty-odd boys—men—for the Senior Shake, pressing hands in the traditional good-bye to lower classmen whose English school designations—third and fourth and fifth form—still confused me even after Whit's four years at Windsor.

when he rose, or shook the headmaster's hand, not when he beamed a triumphant grin in our direction.

"This is for the boys," the senior mother representative said into the microphone, and handed an envelope to the headmaster. Another tradition, this collective donation: the Mothers' Gift. "For new sofas in a commons room," she continued, "or a grill at the pool, or a footbridge at the stream, whatever need arises for the boys." She turned to the audience again. "Would all the mothers please stand up?" The assembly shifted with our rising, and the unexpected request.

"This check is a gift to Windsor School from the mothers, in honor of their sons." She paused and pointed at us. "Look at these mothers. Because not only have we given Windsor this money, we gave you our sons."

Then, tears sprang to my eyes.

A genial dismissing smile from behind the podium, a rustle of seated bodies, sibilant whispers from folded programs. Then, one sudden, high-pitched, giddy and anonymous yelp released them. They surged up from their chairs in an exultant tide, noisy and jubilant, reaching for each other and into breast pockets. Clandestinely purchased cigars were flourished, clipped, and lit, and the acrid scent filled the air above their wide smiles. With clumsy gestures of male affection they clasped each other around the neck, posed triumphantly in the sun for pictures with family, teachers, each other.

I held back, overcome by a roller coaster of emotions: sentiment, euphoria, pride. Pride for his achievements, pride in the number of friends who crowded him, proud of his college acceptance. For my sweetly average boy who'd fretted about his grades, agonized about rejection, and who was rewarded, after all, for being a good citizen who worked hard. Because he earned it, deserved it.

And this small, other pride as well: that he was mine.

Never mind that on this quintessential summer morning identical ceremonies and celebrations were taking place on greener lawns or grander halls or cavernous auditoriums elsewhere. Never mind that ribbon-tied diplomas were being bestowed this day, this hour, upon thousands of high school seniors all over the country. Never mind that this rite had been enacted every June for a hundred Junes at this very school. Because this lawn, this day, this diploma, and this senior, were singularly mine.

Russ clasped Whit's hand firmly and grinned at him as though they were colleagues now. My heart nearly burst for Whit, with love as boundless as the blue heavens above us, and this fleeting thought: *He will never know how much I love him.* I turned to hug Ebie instead, sensing her shy longing to be included in the chaos of celebration.

A plaster cast was suddenly flung heavily around Whit's shoulders. "I came to find you because I don't know when we'll see each other again," a freckled face said earnestly to Whit.

And then my eyes welled a second time, at the boy's unembarrassed show of affection.

⁓

While we finished cramming duffles and boxes and athletic gear into the car, Ebie pawed the graduation gifts. "Look at all your loot," she said of the tokens of remembrance and mutual congratulation. "This one feels like a towel and duh—" she pinched another "—a book." She looked up as Whit thunked his trunk, another relic of mine, down the flight of fire escape stairs.

He was wearing one of his astounding collection of silk-screened T-shirts, a thriving dorm hall industry in an all boys' school. YOU MAY NOT LIKE US, BUT YOUR GIRLFRIEND SURE DOES it read, and I thought again: *Be kind.* Not only to him, with those legions of waiting coeds so easily heartbroken, but to those same legions of girls equally capable of crushing him: *Be tender with him.* "What happened to your graduation clothes?" I asked.

"Shucked 'em."

Yes, as on this day he'd also unknowingly shucked off childhood, and me. Never again would I

SUSAN KELLY

know exactly where he was or what he was doing,
or that he was safe.

We pulled away from the parking lot, drove
slowly past the grand brick buildings with their
stately columns and broad flagstone porticos. Drove
down the long slope of the entrance and past the
empty athletic fields with their acres of clipped grass.
Past the Tin Can, an old gym infrequently used but
for its roof, whose surface the students painted every
autumn with a fresh slogan, a rallying battle cry in
another Windsor ritual. BRING 'EM ON, it had been
emblazoned one year. TAKING ALL COMERS it read
the next autumn.

"FOR GRANT BUT NOT FORGOTTEN," Ebie read
aloud as Russ slowed for a speed bump. "What does
that mean?"

"Grant Reynolds was in our class," Whit said.
"He got cancer when we were juniors, and that's
why we shaved our heads last spring. So when Grant
was bald, we all were, too."

Illness was behind the baldness, then; compassion, not lacrosse. My throat involuntarily tightened.
Oh my paltry, pointless fears, each one unfounded:
tempting fate with early reservations, inclement
weather raining on our graduation day parade, not
attending a first-choice college—

"Is he okay?" Ebie asked Whit.

"He died. This past January."

I looked at the blocky bright orange letters spanning the entire roof, letters large enough to be read from an airplane and certainly from our car windows. The tin glared in the treeless sunshine. FOR GRANT BUT NOT FORGOTTEN. But I had forgotten about Grant Reynolds, who was some mother's child, some mother's son.

And I cried for the third time that day, this time for some mother's sorrow.

Chapter Two

"WITHOUT A FRONT WHEEL IT LOOKS CRIPPLED. OR LIKE it's praying." I spin the rear wheel of Whit's new lightweight collapsible bicycle. Attached to the car roof for the four-hour road trip to the beach, the bike is a graduation present from his grandparents.

Whit lays the detachable front wheel on the back seat. "When I was eleven I wanted a mountain bike for Christmas more than anything," he says, then laughs. "And instead I got a *Huffy*. Ben Harrison teased me forever about it. He'd call me up to go riding and say, 'Bring the Huffy.'"

"You should have told me," I say, struck all these years later that I'd unknowingly embarrassed him, caused him pain instead of pleasure.

Whit adjusts a bungee cord securing the bike to the roof railing. "While we're at the beach I'm going to bungee from that crane near the amusement park at the fishing pier."

"Oh no, you are absolutely not," I say, and add a final bag of groceries to the backseat of my own car. Whit and I are caravanning eastward together.

"I'll use my own paycheck to pay. Or what's left of it. Who's FICA, anyway?"

"The Feds," Russ says. "Your friendly IRS."

"Don't I get a break since my father owns the company I work for?" Whit asks, insulted by the governmental assault of automatically withdrawn taxes. He's working for Lucas Construction this summer, as courier, carpenter, cleaner, and occasionally even roofer. Maybe that explains the current fascination with heights. "Can't you pull any strings, Dad?" he asks.

"Uncle Sam doesn't recognize any benefits of nepotism," Russ laughs. "Welcome to the NFL, pal."

I lean into the car, cram the creased map into the glove compartment, snap the door shut on the crowded contents, and announce again: "No bungeeing."

Russ twangs the antenna spire. "You sure you want to drive by yourself?"

"I drove to the beach last summer when we went."

"But I was in the front seat beside you," I say.

Whit laughs. "Yep, and every time I braked you braced yourself against the dashboard. We need a second car at the cottage, Dad. I've had my license for two years, and besides, I won't be by myself, I'll have Mom in the *lane* beside me."

"Why don't you take the back roads to the coast? It's not as dull as the interstate."

"Because getting stuck behind tobacco tractors on the back route is dull, too," Whit says, "Besides, those back roads make me feel like I'm in *Deliverance* territory."

"The interstate is safer," I add. "If you have car trouble, more cars come by."

"And more cops," Whit grins, and jerks a thumb at me. "She's the one with two tickets on her record. Mom's turning into The Little Old Lady from Pasadena."

"Who?" Ebie asks.

"Never mind. Did you pack stationery for your graduation thank-you notes?"

"And did you pack your James Taylor tapes?" he teases me.

"Seriously, Whit, it's July, a month since you graduated."

"Yes, Laura, they're all finished," he answers with the polite ennui of henpecked sitcom husbands, then high-fives the windshield and reverts to teenagerese. "I am so on task!"

"I addressed all the envelopes for him," Ebie says, "because he told me he'd drive me to Target if I did."

Whit shoots her a look. "Traitor."

"Such a deal," I say. "Signal to me if you want to stop somewhere for a Coke."

"I already know where I want to stop: South of the Border."

"Haven't you outgrown that yet?" I ask, even as I recall how I'd longed to stop there as a child. I'd wanted to pull off the road beside a cotton field when we drove east as well, amazed by the pure white tufts atop gangly, ugly brown stems, begging my parents to *please stop, stop, please let me feel it*.

"All my life, every year we go to the beach, I have asked, no, *begged*, to stop at South of the Border. 'Siesta all day, fiesta all night,'" Whit quotes.

"And no doing your face thing," I warn.

Even the mention makes Ebie laugh. For years of family road trips Whit has entertained himself and the rest of us by mashing his face against the window—his lips and eyes and cheeks stretched and contorted and flattened as though someone were pushing him against the glass—simply to get a reaction from motorists in the next lane.

"The McCalls said they'd pick you up around five," I remind Russ. Every summer since our children were babies we've shared a rental beach cottage with Anne and Craig. Because Whit and I are both taking cars—because he was so determined to take his own—Russ and Ebie will drive down with Anne and Craig later today, so that Russ can finish up at the office and Ebie can go to a birthday party. "Ebie's all packed."

Whit pitches a water bottle on the passenger seat of his car and makes a face at his sister. "I see the beach first, I see the beach first!"

"I don't care," Ebie scowls. "We have a whole week at the beach, and Melissa's only having her birthday at Water Jungle once."

"Put on some sunscreen," I remind her. "And don't forget to bring it with you. Plus the camera."

"Has it been used since graduation?" Russ asks. "Probably needs charging."

"See you tonight," Whit says.

I let him lead the way to the interstate, merge, content to lag behind him and watch neighboring drivers, to try to figure out their lives and personalities from their bumper stickers and vanity license tags and rearview mirror ornaments and back dash clutter—tissue boxes, Beanie Babies. They remind me of one of Whit's driver's ed stories.

My driver's ed instructor is an ex-paramedic. One time he was called to a wreck and they couldn't figure out how it happened. Turned out the man had one of those bobble-head dogs on his back dash and when he braked the toy flew forward and hit him right in the skull where you go unconscious, so he wrecked.

Oh, Whit, please!

It's true. And more people wreck while they're sneezing than any other time.

Raleigh isn't far enough down the road from Greensboro or breakfast, and I let the exit for the Farmer's Market go by. But no one does a vegetable plate like their dome-ceilinged, cheap-as-dirt restaurant—squash with onions, fried okra, candied yams, lima beans. Maybe on the way back. I hope I packed my salad dressing somewhere in the bags of groceries so we won't be forced to use store-bought and hope I tucked my rib sauce recipe somewhere in the dozen issues of magazines I brought to catch up. One night we'll have ribs on the grill, one night we'll go out, one night we'll have a shrimp boil, one night we'll—I stop thinking and look at the speedometer and try to set a good example.

The teacher told us that if a hay bale falls off a truck and you're driving behind it and wreck, it's still your fault.

That doesn't seem fair.

That's what I said. And he said, Suppose a deer jumped into the road. Would you try to sue the deer? The Wildlife Federation? Never brake for an animal. And always look out for the other guy.

That one's been around forever.

Poor Whit, with no cruise control on that car.

At least he doesn't have to deal with changing gears on the flat straightaway of the interstate.

Turn around and tell the car behind me to back up! We're on a hill and when the light changes I'm going to roll backward because I'm not good yet at doing clutch and brake and gas all at the same time. It's not funny!

Another reason to take the interstate. No stoplights, no hills.

I listen to "Out of Africa," wonder what he's listening to, notice a stranded motorist on the shoulder and phone the highway patrol on my cell to report the mile marker whereabouts, my good Samaritan deed of the day. On either side of the road are vast outlet malls, small cities built entirely around the lure and promise of bargains on towels, shoes, china. I check my rearview mirror, see the grill of his Honda, the silhouette of his curls behind the steering wheel. He'd tried to mash them down for his license photograph.

Youwannabeanorgandonor.
What?
The officer picked a piece of lint from her gray uniform and repeated the question in the same bored monotone: Youwannabeanorgandonor.
Say yes, Whit, I said. You want to be an organ donor.
I tap the steering wheel in time with the music,

and lose track of him as drivers cut into the front and the back where the freeway merges and joins I-95. Whit pulls into the lane beside me, grins as he puts on sunglasses.

Check out that guy's shades beside us.
Is he cool?
Thinks he is. See that rainbow flag decal on the car bumper?
Does that mean they're Grateful Dead fans?
Mom. Dancing bears are for Deadheads. Rainbows are for gays.
Oh.

There they are, the familiar, ubiquitous South of the Border billboards, spaced a mile apart for forty miles, then half a mile, then every quarter, then as frequently as the old Burma Shave ads, though a hundred times their size. Evidently, quantity not quality is their marketing motto. Black backgrounds with garish neon letters blaze low-humor hucksterisms in pseudo-Spanish that are cheerfully irresistible. PEDRO'S FORECAST: CHILI TODAY, HOT TAMALE. Fluffy, cartoon lambs spin endlessly, electrically, around a water wheel: YOUR SHEEP ARE ALL COUNTED WEETH PEDRO. A ten-foot hot dog wrapped around with the slogan YOU NEVER SAUSAGE A PLACE—YOU'RE ALWAYS A WIENER AT PEDRO'S. All promote the sprawling

Mexican-themed travel complex—restaurants, motels, carnival rides, gift stores—that straddles the state line. Now and then the signs stoop to pure advertising: PECAN ROLLS, whatever they are, and THE LOWEST CIGARETTE PRICES IN THE CAROLINAS and RESERVATIONS FOR DISNEY/ORLANDO AREA. Oh, here's a new one, an enormous pink gullet behind a set of crooked Chiclet-white teeth: KEEP SCREAMING, KIDS, THEY'LL STOP! it advises, and Whit passes me, pointing and grinning. I shake my head and mouth, "Dairy Queen."

"This is wax, not chocolate," I say as Whit waits for his own dip cone.

He immediately bites off the picture-pretty curved tip from his monster cone. "Have you ever noticed that if there's something in the road—a pothole, or a piece of tire—you can't help steering right for it? It's like a reflex, or an instinct, to head straight for it."

"Thank the truckers for the retreads." Now my tip goes—why not? The hardened coating is the only thing keeping the soft vanilla cream from collapsing. If you lick from the bottom, like a normal cone, it's dripping on your hands in an instant. "Have *you* ever noticed how when you pass a truck they seem to draw you into their speed vacuum, the way it is when a ship goes down?"

"Just keep your legs off the dash when you're passing truckers, Mom."

We laugh. Russ hates for me to perch my feet on the dashboard because he's convinced that in their high cabs truck drivers are looking at me—up me— in their oversized rearview mirrors. "Ready to go again?" I ask. "Can you drive and eat?" As answer, Whit simultaneously pats his nodding head and rubs his stomach.

BACK UP PEDRO, YOU MEESED IT! entreats the billboard before us on the interstate as we encounter the work zone on a stretch of seemingly perpetual highway construction, with concrete dividing barricades and blinking speed signals and raised grids of white lines that tug and grip the car's tires like the grooved steel of a drawbridge. In hopes of deterring speeders, the same defunct trooper cars are parked in the median as last summer, bearing the same stuffed dummies complete with hat and uniform behind the steering wheel.

Whit pulls into the lane beside me, points to the imposters, and rolls his jaded eyes as we ride into the humid remnants of a summer thunderstorm. A whitish smear trails the rear door of his car and I laugh, knowing his cone had disintegrated before he'd finished the ice cream, and he'd thrown it outside the window. The spitty rain is less hindrance than nuisance, hard enough only to force an annoying, occasional touch to the one-swipe windshield wipers. Drivers cut into and merge and change

lanes without benefit of signal where two other free-
ways join I-95, and I avoid the obvious road-ragers
and speed demons and eighteen-wheel-truck
jockeys who nevertheless manage to box me within
their silvery-sided walls.

So that I lose sight of a small compact used automobile bought with his own money, thanks to graduation gifts and despite FICA, a grayish import the
identical color of rain and road and guardrails and
truck siding and tire-thrown vapor and the tractionless compound of oil and water.

You don't see it happen. You don't hear anything
either, not with the rushing trucks and the hiss of
rain and Jimmy Buffet going down easy as a mar-
garita. In my rearview mirror and sideview mirrors
the curly head vanishes. He was stowing sunglasses or
reaching for the radio or the wiper button or . . .

He is simply, suddenly, not there.

Chapter Three

YOU'VE SEEN THEM, SPED PAST THEM, THOSE MAKESHIFT
roadside memorials. For years I couldn't decide
whether those highway altars were ghoulish or
ridiculous: stalky wire legs supporting florist circles,
cellophane flapping over a photograph, a tattered
American flag, a white cross stark against undergrowth. Sometimes the crosses are puffy-looking,
swollen with crimped plastic or bubble wrap.
Recently I've noticed plaster of Paris and concrete
angels perched beside the wreaths of permanent
flowers. Angels are in.

Here is what you think. You think if you can get
them past the conventional childhood perils, past
drowning, past drinking Lysol, past closing themselves up inside refrigerators, past getting run over on
their bikes on the way to school, that you are free and

clear. "It was like a dream, Mom," he'd said with soft stunned wonder. His body was curled on the buttoned ticking of the bare mattress, and unnaturally still for an eight-year-old. I'd stripped his sheets, and sent him to school on his bicycle, and he hadn't looked both ways and an elderly man driving an elderly sedan had sideswiped him.

"Like a dream," he'd whispered slowly again, and I'd stopped then, in my chores, and realized the terror that gripped him now, in the aftermath. Now that he was living again.

You think of all the freakish tragedies reported by friends or the media in low tones or loud headlines: children snatched in mall parking lots, their hair cut in restroom stalls, false phone calls placed to no known number to show the child that his parents don't want him back. The child killed by copperheads nesting in the plastic ball pen at a fast-food restaurant. The child who fell from the unscreened fifth-story apartment window to concrete. The child crushed beneath a crate loosed from a forklift's grip at Toys 'R' Us as he and his father stood near the delivery entrance waiting to pick up his newly assembled bike.

You remember each instance of incaution and inattention lying there for death's taking, when you might have been punished and were spared. When he woke at four a.m. night after night for a period when he was three, and you, exhausted beyond patience, sat him in the middle of the floor with a cut-up orange and said, "Fine, stay up by yourself. I'm going back to bed," when he might have crawled and fallen head-first down the stairs or licked an electric socket. When you failed to give him antibiotics before a dentist appointment though he had a heart murmur and might have developed a lethal infection. When you left him for a weekend with the babysitter you scarcely knew. When you argued with him about a meningitis vaccination recommended for anyone living in dorm situations. How he hadn't wanted it, knew it would hurt, and how you'd said, "Wouldn't you rather sting for minute than die?"

You remember the days when you fussed at him, needing and wanting him to nap so you could stretch your legs in the sun, thinking *Go to sleep, hurry, before the good tan time is over!* You remember the weekends when his friends crowded every room, and you; the basketball games in the driveway and your trampled flowerbeds from fouls, the Kool-Aid stains on the counters and the empty soda bottles, weekends when a meal couldn't be planned because he was playing his social options, when you longed for Monday, and peace, and normalcy. You remember the days when there were so many appliances churning or ringing or blaring—phone, music, television, washer, dryer—that you couldn't hear yourself think, and now there is nothing but silence in which to listen to yourself think.

You remember all the times you complained when he slapped the moldings above the doors—coming down the stairs, walking into the kitchen—a habit of height. And there they are still, four smudges of his fingers. You go into the downstairs bathroom and see the ceiling fan cover askew and remember how it once irritated you that his roughhousing in the room above, thumping and falling to the floor with his father or sister, would shake loose the fan cover. Now you cry at the sight of it, and nod your head *yes* when your husband comes home, sees your face and your eyes and says, "Another landmine?" because every day, every conversation and magazine article and errand are riddled with sabotage. Even the *thwack* of newspaper landing on the driveway at the pre-dawn hour when the rest of the world—but not you—is still unconscious, is sabotage. A reminder that everyone else has gone on living.

"Sun's out," he would call from his crib too early on weekend mornings, when he was old enough to want out, down, up. "I hungy."

You remember how he phoned from Windsor on Sunday nights and said in all seriousness, "Mom, it's Whit," as if you wouldn't know. How, when you dropped him off that first September you cried all the way to the state line on the way home, melodramatically telling your husband, "The next time we see him, he'll be engaged!"

But that was a temporary absence. This absence is forever.

You wonder how you will ever fill the dishwasher. You gaze at a broccoli bunch and wonder how your family ever used to eat an entire head. You open the drawer where the placemats are stacked as they were last put away, four of the blue plaid on top until two weeks later when the pattern is reestablished, only three of the blue plaid on top, only three of the straw ovals. Unless you burrow to the bottom, where the old yellow laminates are still nestled in a group of four. When there were still four in your family.

You remember every worthless irresponsibility you scolded him for; every unmade bed or paper on the floor; the candy wrappers and orthodontic elastics floating out of the dryer from pants pockets, or Chapstick tubes scoured hollow, their waxy contents melted away. You remember giving him a new Chapstick in every Christmas stocking, not permitting him to root around in your handbag to use yours. How he'd laughed when he'd recently told you, "I used to stand over the trash can when I ate cookies so crumbs wouldn't drop on the floor."

You do laundry and yearn for a crumpled sodden pack of matches to fall from an inside-out pocket to make you anxious about whether—and what—he was smoking. You remember him putting his face in a freshly laundered towel and saying, "Oh, it smells so good."You put away the clean clothes and wish you had a reason to open his drawers and frown at the heap of unmatched socks that you'd fussed he used and discarded as carelessly as tissues.

You unreasonably hold things against people. How they worded their sympathy notes. Against strangers in the supermarket line grousing about their college-age children. *"I couldn't get hold of her. What is she doing at two o'clock in the morning?"* Each innocent complaint is a barbed arrow. *"I had his ass for overdrawing." "What does he need a microwave for?"* Even against the mailman who delivers futilely threatening form letters for him from a CD mail order club. Even against your mother, for once thoughtlessly, blithely telling you, "This is the hardest thing you will ever go through," when you were dumped by a boyfriend twenty years ago. You hear of a college freshman who overdosed on Benadryl and you think, *Yes, but he had a year more than mine.*

You wander about his room still cluttered with belongings so recently unpacked, and then under duress. Remember how, after you replaced the carpeting and the quilts when he went to boarding school, added an actual drinking glass in the bathroom instead of the accordion'd collapsible cup he'd taken to camp, he'd said, "This place looks more like a guest room than *my* room."

Not to you it doesn't. Because you study the

graduation presents, still new, and turn them over in your hands. Two money clips, a monogrammed towel, a pocketknife, an answering machine. A set of nesting coolers. A stadium chair. A glass paperweight bearing the Windsor school logo. A letter opener, a de rigueur Cross pen that would soon have been lost. A suede frame in hunter green in which he'd stuck a photograph of the faculty-grad softball team. Too recent, too heartbreaking, those boys to men so recent, too. Oversized mugs in crystal and Lucite and classic vanilla porcelain with his to-be collegiate crest. A pewter Jefferson cup or mint julep cup, whatever it is, useless as the pewter cigar holder. A canvas carryall. A monogrammed sterling belt buckle from his grandmother, and Tiffany.

You open the closet door and breathe in the aroma of his clothes, still scented with the overly sweet, overly false, overly citrusy fragrance of room deodorizers purchased in the Windsor student store and stuck to dorm closet walls to offset the stink of sweaty sneakers and unwashed clothing. You're fearful that the slightly sickening smell you once longed to dissipate will, all too soon, do just that.

Your fingers move along the shelves to the school projects, the papier-mâché tribal mask, the gallon jar full of matchbooks, the roll of duct tape whose thick silvery lengths he used on everything from hems to sunglasses to backpacks. You stroke the spines of

unread classics, move along to the Boy Scout hand-
book, the card trick book, the slender pamphlet of
harmonica lessons, the book about human freaks—
Elephant Man and Tiny Tim. You touch the stray toy,
the Transformer, buildings into bugs or vice versa,
insects into aliens, He-man and Skeletor, the heroes
and villains of his childhood. The bead necklace from
Adele McCall, my godchild, draped over the lamp-
shade that you'd warned him might melt, catch fire,
still dangling too near to a light bulb that no longer
needs to burn. All of these possessions, transformed
from ordinary objects to relics, are still there in his
room. He is not.

And the pins: shortened, clipped, blunted straight
pins in a square frame that permits you to press them
against anything and make an impression that lasts
until you invert it, and restore the pins to a single
layer. A tactile plaything, cool and prickly against the
skin, impossible to put down. There it is, his face-on
face, the lips and eyes and nose and chin outlined in
silver-shadowed three-dimensional relief, a mask of
his features as though he were an Egyptian prince. A
single flick and the pins will drop and he'll be gone,
and the plaything's temporal nature so terrifies you
that you slide it—hide it—behind *Robin Hood* and
King Arthur and the confirmation Holy Bible, books
you know no one will disturb.

You dread five to seven in the evening, the

hardest time, just as it once was. "The Arsenic Hour" Anne used to call it, when there were fretting babies, then tired toddlers, then extracurricular activity car pools and hurried suppers, the last-minute trip to the library or trying to dress before dashing to an evening meeting. The Arsenic Hour is now the Empty Hour. This is evolution.

And here is what you do after he's gone: nothing.

You don't see them anymore, those clever plastic steering wheels—complete with beeping center horn and oversized key and turn signals—that attached to toddler car seats. No doubt someone deemed them unsafe. But you still see those roadside shrines—a brightly colored blotch of a deflated helium balloon tied to a teddy bear, a piece of clothing, an angel—sanctuaries slowly disintegrating in the sun and the rain and the wind and the grit.

You've seen them. They mark the moment when everything that *is* becomes *was* and all you *are* becomes *were* and past tense in an instant becomes permanent and eternal. They mark somebody's baby, somebody's darling, somebody's child.

Mine.

Chapter Four

FOR TWENTY YEARS MY NEIGHBOR AND I HAVE LIVED twenty feet from each other and haven't exchanged twenty words.

"Here," Mrs. Matheny said at my front door the day we moved in, and held out her version of a welcome-to-the-neighborhood gift: a Stouffer's casserole still frozen inside the orange box. She didn't bring anything when Whit died. But how would she have known? We don't speak. I don't know her first name.

"Tell your son not to throw his ball over here," she said once over the split-rail fence that separates our front lawn from hers. As though emphasizing her point, an ugly spiky pampas grass plant keeps sentry on her side of the fence.

"She's the meanest lady in the world," Whit said. "Meany Matheny."

"She's afraid he'll get hurt in her yard and she'll have to pay the insurance," Anne told me. Anne and Darrell live at the end of Liberty Avenue, where our street is shaded by a long line of towering oaks. Anne and I once patrolled that area, a posse of two chasing away the parked cars of soccer moms on cell phones killing time between car pools, noontime office workers eating lunch, sunbathers bound for the grassy open park beyond. "Your car crushes the tree roots," we told them.

Upstairs, Ebie's door opened. "When's supper?" she called.

If I were upstairs in the bedroom instead of in the kitchen, I'd see that Mrs. Matheny's curtains are closed for the night. She draws them before dusk has even fallen. "Twenty minutes."

"She can't hear that," Russ said, coming into the kitchen. "Twenty minutes!" he shouted.

"That's a small eternity!" Ebie yelled back. "I might as well practice the piano."

Whit's phrase. But there are no small eternities any more. Just eternities.

Along our backyard's boundary with Mrs. Matheny is another fence. Not a friendly fence painted white, or a modestly charming weathered split-rail but a strictly serviceable board divider. Russ asked the Mathenys if they were interested in sharing the cost of a fence that would look attractive on their side, too, but they said no. Mrs. Matheny's husband was alive then. So was Whit.

So we suited ourselves with an inexpensive, affordable version: narrow pointed slats that reminded me of the stockade walls at Jamestown. While Russ was installing it, Whit, who was seven, had accidentally stumbled into an underground wasp's nest hidden beneath the ivy. "Strip off all their clothes," a doctor had told me about a toddler who shrieks uncontrollably. Whit was stung seven times. But he lived.

I have no relationship with Mrs. Matheny, but I know she opens her bedroom curtains soon after nine in the morning. I watch her make her bed and place her corduroy backrest against the wall. Then the light goes on in the bathroom window, and I see her gray head near a wicker wall shelf. Then, wearing slippers and a navy blue velour robe, she goes out to get her newspaper.

I opened the dishwasher, saw the crusted remains of Tuesday's spaghetti on plates. "I don't like the way glasses feel when they come out of the dishwasher," Whit said to me once. "Too clean. Dry and squeaky." I knew what he meant. I wish someone would ask me *What do you miss?* I'd say *His observations.* "The ivy needs a haircut," he'd say. Or, "Tears in your throat are hard as bullets."

No one asks what I miss. Instead they ask—

"What did you do today?" Russ asked.

Anne has voiced the same question, or a version of it. "What are you doing inside all day, cleaning house?" she joked. "Remember that time you found so many pubic hairs all over Ebie's bathroom and then realized she'd given her African-American doll a haircut?"

But that's the problem: remembering. "See you in heaven!" I said to my children when we drove over a long drawbridge or at the crest of a roller coaster hill, and they cheerily answered back.

See you in heaven!

"I . . ." What I did today was watch. Watched from the bedroom window. Watched the street, the houses, the driveways, the lawn below me. The lawn where Whit had accidentally let go of a helium balloon, mutely observed it float above the roofline and the trees until he'd finally shouted, "God! Send it back!"

God! Send him back!

"Tell your ivy to stay out of my yard," I should have told Mrs. Matheny the way she warned me about Whit. Mrs. Matheny's rampant ivy long ago took over both fences, draping them with a viney curtain. Unless I strip it from the trunks, the ivy will choke our trees too. Mrs. Matheny doesn't like trees. I feel her silent hatred of my pin oak.

When she had her pecan tree taken down, Whit

and I watched from the same window I watch from now. We suffered at the destruction of a magnificent, innocent tree for no better reason than its unthinkable audacity of dropping leaves on her yard every autumn. We endured the day-long ratchet and clatter of saws and chippers, the sight of hacked limbs chopped and stacked, the flat, naked, rawly yellow stump. By midafternoon, fifty years of growing, shading, and shedding had been reduced to a pile of shavings finer than sawdust. Not even useful for mulch, but vacuumed away. Our house seemed to cower and squint and shrink from sudden, unexpected exposure, before I got used to the extra sunlight. "You can get used to anything," people blithely joke, "even a hanging." But you don't get used to a dead child.

When you watch for long periods, tears don't necessarily fall. They collect, and sit in your eyes, and recede, then well up again. I told Russ that someone should add it to the song: The sad bone connected to the tear duct. He looked at me as though I'd lost my mind.

"She washed her car again today," I said and turned up the heat under the pasta water. To prove I haven't lost my mind and can make conversation. To prove to Russ I'm not . . . depressed. I'm not depressed. What I am is just . . . waiting for something. "I think she details cars as a sideline." To prove I still have a sense of humor.

"Who?"

"The fitness freak." She addressed my garden club on the topic of personal fitness once. Back when I went to meetings.

"Who?" he asked again, and reached for the pretzel bag on top of the refrigerator.

"I don't know her name. Across and two doors down." Spandex'd in brilliant colors, she rides her bike away on some sunny days. Other sunny days she brings buckets and rags and a portable vacuum to her driveway. I watch her shine hubcaps, polish the interior rear window, omitting nothing. Then she lies in the front yard tanning on a chaise.

I took three glasses from the cabinet. Only three. "It's too late to get a tan," I said to Russ. Yesterday I'd opened the door to Ebie's room too soon after knocking and as she modestly darted for cover, I glimpsed pale flashes of flesh against the fading summer tan. When did Ebie get a tan? We never made it to the beach.

"Isn't it too late? In September?" To show Russ that I knew what month it was.

"Were we talking about tans?" he asked.

The June that Whit planted pumpkin and watermelon seeds in the back where the sun falls unshaded, Mrs. Matheny rudely told him, "We used to have a garden, too. It was right where your house is."

We used to have Deep Woods, Whit's name for

the undeveloped acreage behind our house. "I'm building a fort in the Deep Woods, Mom," he'd say. "We're playing army in the Deep Woods." The Deep Woods have been recently tamed and civilized, planted with grass and mowed regularly. Open and graded, it's now easy to envision the land as lots.

"All this property was wooded," Mrs. No-First-Name Matheny told Whit. "There's just that left." At least I can understand her resentment now, given what's happening in Winwood, on Liberty Avenue.

Russ picked up a jar of pasta sauce, a bag of broccoli florets. "Are we having another supper out of a kit?"

Before Mrs. Matheny's ivy obliterated it, we had a natural area in our back yard. Spring bulbs pushed through the pine needles and I have photographs of Whit in powder blue corduroy overalls crouching beside the bright yellow heads of King Alfred daffodils. But for the pictures, I wouldn't be able to remember a time when the ivy, deep and thick and green-black, wasn't there. It has crept stealthily from her yard into ours, sprouting among the pachysandra, around our air-conditioning unit, twining into the nandina no matter how often I yank it out. You think you can battle ivy and win, but you can't. It always wins.

"Laura," Russ said, and uncorked a bottle of wine.

"You're wearing a tie." There. That's a thought. He doesn't usually wear a tie to work.

"I had a meeting." He loosened the tie and I began to set the table and waited for him to say it: *You have to move on.*

I know what I'm doing. I know the names for it. Avoidance. Denial. Watching lets me avoid and deny the absence that accosts me in a dozen daily, relentless, inanimate details.

I watch the driveway where he learned to ride a two-wheeler, frantically trying to keep the wobbling bicycle upright as he veered toward the street while I called, "Pedal! Keep pedaling! Keep moving!"

You have to keep moving, Russ will say. But no. "Did you call the psychologist?" he asked instead.

"Yes."

I did do that, I did. Because Ebie has begun tugging at the hairs on her arms. Separating the tiny strands with her fingernails and pulling them out. Or circling her fingers over and over them, until the skin is raw.

"And?"

"She said it's unconscious, a habit. She said . . . she said it's because Whit's gone."

"Of course it is."

I traced the groove in a fork's bamboo handle. *Of course* is Whit's clothing folded and waiting to be worn in his drawers, supposing that his life would just go on uninterrupted, unblighted. Nothing is *of course* anymore. Nothing.

"She said to have Ebie wear long sleeves when she reads at night," I told Russ, "so her fingers will touch fabric when she reaches for her arms, and remind her of what she's doing. And to have her wear gloves to sleep because she's probably lying in bed and pulling her arm hair out without even being aware that she's doing it." Grief is like that, a huge magnet pulling and pinning you to one place, making you heavy, heavy.

Jutting from beneath the cutlery tray as I gather three forks are coupons for free french fries and frozen yogurt given as good-behavior rewards after dentist or doctor appointments. Even their presence pierces me, that they were tucked away and forgotten and left to expire. All those treats I left unredeemed.

Expired. Even the verbs. Even the everyday language.

Among the scraps of paper in the drawer I'd found his handwriting on a note: *I went to get a haircut.* Like the ivy on the fence needs a haircut, as he once said. Sometimes I watch the ivy instead of Mrs. Matheny and her house. I've seen a rabbit on its hind legs, still as a statue, and felt certain his beaded black eye watched mine. Friend or foe? it asked. Watch little daily dramas outside my window, the squirrels rustling, foraging, scampering in the photinia branches, a pair of cardinals attacking a fat-cheeked chipmunk scuttering in the mass of ivy vines, the cat who sits utterly silent, utterly alert on the ivied fence, tail curling slowly, with all the time in the world to pensively study the ivy. Just like me.

"Look at me, Laura," Russ said patiently, and I did. I love him, but he's the kind of man who can take the mail from the slot and put it on the counter without even looking at it. "So what?" Anne has said cheerfully. "All Darrell and I talk about are our calendars."

Yes. The days just keep coming at you.

Mrs. Matheny had a husband, too. When she mowed the yard he'd sit on their front stoop beneath a twirling wind decoration made of tiny mirrors and Popsicle sticks.

"He's Hawaiian," Anne told me. "He survived Pearl Harbor by hiding in an oil drum."

Whit had been enchanted with this information and incorporated it—along with an empty tuna fish can as a substitute oil drum—in his imaginary play with a set of green plastic soldiers in the front yard while I sat on our own stoop, knitting and talking to him.

"I'm playing Army," he'd say. Not playing "soldiers" or "war" or "bad guys." Just Army.

One day there was an ambulance in the Matheny driveway; not flashing, not wailing. Then there were cars for several days, and then I realized the husband had died. Meany Matheny probably doesn't realize Whit is dead.

Dead.

Russ folded the pretzel bag. "Did you and Anne walk today?"

I shook my head. We used to walk, Anne checking her pedometer fastened to the waistband of her leggings. Now I watch other walkers instead, mothers with their strollers, and hear them talking, the occasional blurt of laughter. They talk of their children, their living children. Some walkers I recognize just by their dogs, or gaits, even though I don't know their names. Some of the walkers aren't walkers at all. A man carrying something is either trying to sell soap or subscriptions to prove that he's been successfully rehabbed and has a newfound sense of purpose. Two people on a single bicycle means one of them will ride away on a stolen bike. Sometimes Meany Matheny takes a slow-stepped walk. She wears a straw hat at a stiff, odd angle on her head, like one of those hats donkeys wear in childhood-book illustrations, with slits cut out for their ears.

"You should keep a tally of Winwood walking fashions," Anne has said, "as much as you stand at that window."

I could: Martha Donald in her capri leggings walking her drop-kick dog. Lynn Forrester's turban.

Mrs. Joyner's come-rain-or-come-shine belted trench-coat and plastic rainbonnet. Mrs. Wyatt's tam o'shanter.

"Why don't we take a walk?" Anne asked. "Want to?"

She's tried, Anne; she has. But she says, "You've hardly been outside the house since Whit's accident, Laura."

Accident. As though he'd broken his arm or sliced off a fingertip while he peeled an apple.

Russ handed me the olive oil. "Did you read the Public Records section in the paper today?"

I shook my head again. How could I get to the Public Records section when I couldn't get beyond the Section A filler piece with box charts of automobile accident statistics, neat graphs and columns of daily, weekly, monthly and yearly wrecks and fatalities with subcategories of mitigating factors: drinking, wearing or not wearing seatbelts, presence or absence of driver or passenger-side air bags, their deployment or non-, on and on and meaningless insurance fodder, public service announcement white noise—until that statistic is your statistic.

"The two bungalows at the top of the hill sold," Russ said.

I looked at him. He's a handsome man. When he was younger a stewardess thought he was Superman, Christopher Reeve. He's good with people, good at his job as a contractor. "I never saw a sign."

"Don't even need For Sale signs in Winwood anymore. Word of mouth is all it takes. People are itching to live here."

With its modest homes on big squares of lots like a checkerboard, Winwood seemed a Dick and Jane neighborhood come to life when we moved here twenty years ago. Then, Winwood had a babysitting co-op and new-parent camaraderie and backyard barbecues. The July Fourth parade featured fathers in formation for the Lawn Mower League that stopped for a Diaper Drill, and a local politician rode in a borrowed old broad-bodied Cadillac trailing bunting.

Then, Chippendale planters were *le rage* as Anne calls trends. A splintery pair with rotted crosspieces still adorns the front stoop of a shingled Cape Codder five houses down from us, where an independently wealthy young potter lives.

Winwood fringes Brantley Park, one of those neighborhoods that's always described in newspaper features as *tony* or *wealthy* or *high end*. The proximity to Brantley Park's high-cotton houses have, in twenty years' time, made Winwood itself valuable real estate.

"We ought to rename Winwood Outer Brantley," Anne has joked, "like England's Cotswalds. Upper Slaughter, Lower Slaughter, Greater Edgecomb, Lesser Edgecomb."

These days *le rage* is pairs of evergreen topiary

miniatures: inverted cones, pom-pom triplets in descending orbs, elongated spirals. Except for Mrs. Matheny. Though her husband survived Pearl Harbor, she doesn't so much as put out an American flag on July Fourth. Our American flag was one of Whit's tenth-birthday presents. It's in the coat closet, leaning against the wall beside a card table that he set up to sell lemonade. For his sixteenth birthday we gave him a fly-fishing rod, and for his eighteenth, a shotgun. For his twenty-first I was planning on giving him a beautiful—

"The sale will probably mean more construction," Russ said, "but that's good news for us."

—antique box, with inlay, for the tuxedo studs and cuff links he'd have had one day, and wristwatch, and paper clips, and old keys and golf tees and—

"Good news?" I echoed. It is?

Russ nibbled a piece of uncooked cappellini. "Sure. Raises property values. We all win."

We do?

"Mom," Ebie said from the den door. "What do you want to hear?"

This hasn't changed. Ebie always asked what I wanted her to play when she practiced the piano. "'Edelweiss,'" I answered. "Or 'Beauty and the Beast.' 'Somewhere Over the Rainbow.'"

She rifled through sheet music, sat down at the piano, and the beginning notes of the songs tinkled piquant and plaintively. Even the two-handed melodies were embroidered with the sound of loss.

Russ looked at me. "Ebie," he called, "how about 'Chariots of Fire' instead?" He shook chopped steamed broccoli into the tangle of angel hair. "I'll toss."

"What do you think she does all day long?" I asked him. When the curtains don't open or close on time I invent a life for Meany Matheny. She's gone to spend the night or weekend with a grown child, or her grandchildren, though I've never seen children of any kind in her yard. Once, flowers were delivered to her door after an absence and I knew that she'd been sick.

"Who?"

"Mrs. Matheny."

Russ stopped pulling at the pasta. His expression was a mix of exasperation and anxiety and pity. "Minding her own business, like you should."

But that's all I do, mind my business. I ground pepper over the pale strands, shook salt.

"Did you buy some gloves for Ebie?" he asked.

It's not that I forgot, it's that I just—

"Laura," Russ said gently at my back. "What *did* you do today?"

"I . . ."

I'd opened the screen to let out a trapped wasp. I'd watched Mrs. Matheny reverse her gold sedan slowly onto the street, and wondered where she was going—a hairdresser appointment, the grocery store. I watched her tilt her city trash can and roll it slowly up the hill. She gets to go on living.

Russ put down the tongs, bodily turned me, and held both my wrists in his hands. "Maybe she sits inside and looks out the window and wonders what *you* do all day."

It takes no effort to pare your life to nothing, to cease running errands or making phone calls or volunteering or taking walks or cleaning house. It takes no effort to disconnect. You plug in the answering machine, and stand at the window, and monitor the comings and goings of your changing neighborhood where lots have become more valuable than the houses that occupy them.

"I called the psychologist," I told him. "I brought in the trash can that . . ."

I brought in the trash can from beside the culvert where Whit had waited for the school bus one Monday morning. On a Cub Scout weekend trip to Charleston he'd purchased a genuine Confederate cannon ball with his saved allowance—"My own money," he put it importantly—at a museum souvenir shop. He'd put the cannon ball carefully in a paper bag to take to second grade Show and Tell. As I washed breakfast dishes I watched then, too, from the kitchen window, as my son waited excitedly for the bus. I watched as the paper bag split and the cannon ball dropped heavier than any stone into the culvert six feet deep below a grid of thick iron bars, utterly irretrievable.

Watched his eyes widen and fill in disbelief and horror and sadness at the enormous unfairness of it. *Send it back.* No doubt the cannon ball is there to this day. Unlike Whit.

I cannot bear it, cannot stand it. I cannot. But I do. Stand and watch.

"You need to . . ." Russ began. "You have got to stop obsessing about that woman. You have got to function, and stop living like this."

You have got to stop being incredulous, Russ said to me when Whit left his blazer at church three Sundays in a row. *You have got to stop being incredulous,* Russ said when Whit spent all his allowance on a piggy bank shaped like an oversized silver dime. *You have got to stop being incredulous,* Russ said yet again when I discovered that Whit had waited until the evening before the due date to begin writing a fifth grade social studies report on the Sioux Indians. *It's just being a boy,* Russ said. *That's the way boys are.*

"You've got to stop . . ." He hesitated.

Unshed tears in your throat are hard, solid bullets. Whit was right. "Stop missing him?"

"This . . . brooding." Russ pushed himself away

from the counter. "Ebie needs you, Laura." He placed the pasta on the table. "Come back to us."

Come back. I took the salad from the refrigerator and remembered how, out of Whit's hearing, Russ and I had laughed long and hard over the final lines of Whit's report: *At the Battle of the Little Bighorn the Sioux were soundly defeated. So far they have not made a comeback.* We had howled so, even later, in bed. So far they have not made a comeback.

Like Whit.

Russ drank his wine. "I miss you, too. Ebie and I are still here."

But Whit is not.

"Ebie?" I called. Loud enough this time. "Supper." I sat down and opened my napkin. "But I am here, Russ." You can have a neighbor and not be one. You can live in a neighborhood, and love it, and still not be *of* it. "I'm here all the time."

Chapter Five

I HAD A TREELESS CHILDHOOD, SO I CHERISH THEM. TREES ask for nothing, provide so much: pools of shade, gnarled roots for pretend play, branches for climbing. A steady presence, benevolently invincible. And in autumn, the grace of falling leaves.

The hand-shaped poplar leaves are first to yellow, and fall. Then the diminutive dogwoods grow crimped and reddish, almost polite in their shedding, as though they're embarrassed to lose their foliage. Pin oaks linger stubbornly into January, when autumn hasn't only lost its charm but vanished as a season altogether. Depending on the date and the weather, leaves waft earthward in infinite variety: float singly, flutter steadily, pour down, or are ripped away by wind. Fallen leaves have transformed my yard from solid green to a speckled carpet in the single day— yesterday, a Sunday—when I wasn't watching because

I was too ill with a hangover. There are a finite
number of days the leaves fall and I'd missed one, lost
it. Somehow, too, I'd missed seeing the invitation—
the reason behind the hangover—slid under our
door two weeks earlier. "Accidentally on purpose,"
Whit would have said.

But Russ had found it, and read it aloud.

Autumn Block Party!
Come join your neighbors for an evening of fun.
Bring a covered dish. A-J vegetable/salad.
K-R chips/bread. S-Z dessert.
Date: October 25. Time: 7:30 p.m.
Place: 522 Liberty Ave-to-be. No rain date.

"Great idea," he'd said. "It's the house under construction. Just been framed in so the party's on the
subflooring. Ready-made dance floor, nothing to
ruin. Know which one?"

I knew which one, though it seemed every third
house on Liberty Ave was under some type of construction. Small projects—dormers where there was
only a slanted roof, new kitchen cabinets, a replaced
porch railing—blossomed overnight into full-blown
remodeling, as though owners shrugged and said,
With all the mess we might as well do the bath-
rooms, too. New kitchens, new entrances, new sun
rooms, new garages, new second stories. And new

entire houses as well: three two-bedroom cottages have been sold and are being replaced with two new and bigger homes.

"'522 Liberty Ave-to-be,'" Russ read. "Get it? 'To be'?"

I stood at my dresser and picked through earrings in a porcelain ashtray, a wedding present. I slid two golden hoops down my index finger, plucked out a pair of brushed-silver stars. When had I ever worn such . . . *large* earrings?

"We need to get out of the house," Russ went on, pinching the skin between his brows. "For some . . . social distraction and interaction." He chuckled at his phrasing. "Don't you miss it?"

Dangling teardrop burgundy and ivory beads. Emerald-cut diamond studs that looked every bit as fake as they were. Meeting earrings, cocktail party earrings. They rattled against discarded catalogs as I tossed them in the trash can. I wasn't going to meetings, or to cocktail parties, or to an Autumn Block Party. "You've had social distraction."

"What?"

"On Labor Day, when you smoked cigars with the new neighbors half the night."

Russ made a small gesture. "So? They're nice people. Practically newlyweds."

"Then you go. I don't want to."

"Why not?"

"Because . . ." Because it had been difficult enough listening to a minister say *The Lord has reasons we don't understand, we want to question, we want to turn away from Him.* How do they make it fresh, every funeral? How do they summon the emotion? "Because of what they say and how they act."

"Who's 'they'?"

"People." *You're in our prayers* and *We're thinking of you.* The elaborate politeness. *This hard time*, they say, *This transition.* Transition?

"People are trying to be nice, Laura. They try to show compassion and you hold it against them. What would you like them to say?"

"I . . ." I'd like them to say, *How do you even get dressed every morning? How do you stand it?*

Russ brought two socks to my window to check their color because the closet's overhead light had been burned out for a month, waiting for me to replace it. "They don't mean anything by it."

I held small tortoiseshell ovals to the fading light at my watching window. It was time for supper and Mrs. Matheny hadn't drawn her curtains. That's just it, I thought: They don't mean it.

I didn't mean to get drunk, either.

⁓

Somewhere down Liberty Ave a blower battalion started up, and I quick-stepped into the tool shed to avoid its shrill whine too similar to the painful ringing in my head yesterday.

I used to blow our leaves, the blower attached to the house by a long umbilicus of orange cord. The task reminded me of roller-skating as a child. The preparations were similar: clamping clunky skates onto shoes and tightening with the key seemed related to unspooling the extension cord and plugging it in. The first wobbly strides lengthening into swoops were like growing accustomed to the power of the whooshing air, controlling the machine's gush. And the warm friction of the handle in my palms was like the warm friction of my feet skating on pavement.

Whit and I argued good-naturedly about blowing styles. "Blow from the top," he'd insist. "If you blow from the bottom of the pile the leaves just fly back at you. Then make a line across the yard and work toward the curb."

"No," I'd disagree, laugh. "I like circling around, forming a pile."

Just as with roller-skating, eventually pleasant friction becomes unpleasant itching, and the blower's reassuring hum becomes keening.

⌣

"Why not go to the party?" Anne had said. "Ebie's finally old enough to stay home by herself."

And Whit will never get any older. I stuck four

fingers in four soda bottles, tucked two cereal boxes under my arm, and nudged open the kitchen door with my hip.

Anne called after me on my way to the recycling bin. "What are you supposed to bring?"

"Dessert." A morning glory was still bravely, bluely blooming, its vine curling near the trash can. No frost, not yet. Fall comes slowly to the South, but a clarity to the light, a preciseness of shadows, announced that even if fall wasn't here, summer was over.

Anne looked at the invitation again. "I have vegetable or salad. Ugh. I should have taken notes at garden club. There was this long discussion about what food to take to people. Gayle Lowry actually keeps files! She says it depends on whether someone's celebrating or moving in or has just had a baby or are nursing and can't eat spicy stuff, or need comfort food for—" she caught herself.

Say it, Anne, I thought, *say For funeral food.* Brisk, practical, chop-chop Anne who'd said to me, "You need to get back into the patterns of your life. Come to garden club."

I looked across our yard to Mrs. Matheny's and remembered the frozen Stouffer's casserole. Mrs. Matheny should have gone to garden club. This fall there was no *chicka-chicka-chicka-chicka* of October watering, the stuttering type-A sprinklers. I preferred the sway and patter of the gentle arcing sprinklers, the kind that I'd played in as a child, more like actual raindrops, and blessedly quiet. But a summer drought had strained the community's water supply, and we were on voluntary water restriction.

Still, though, everyone was at it, reestablishing their lawns and the patterns of their life, as Anne suggested I do. They hired crews to rake and aerate and seed yards left patchy and pathetic after the thatcher's noisy onslaught scraped away the brittle mat of exhausted summer grass, so that lawns were left raw as a child's skinned knee.

Everyone, that is, except us. Unlike the grass, housing starts were up and Russ was too busy to reseed. "Did they talk about aerating and germination?"

Anne leaned against the kitchen steps banister. "Huh?"

I'd looked across the street where fertilizer granules crushed beneath tires had left white starbursts on the driveway. The yard was littered with cylindrical pellets of earth like dog turds, the aerator's by-product. "At garden club."

Anne peered at me a long moment, sighed. "Not at my table." She folded her invitation neatly into fourths and put it in her jeans pocket. "Just do box brownies, Laura. They're easy."

I found the rake in the tool shed, behind the bulb

digger and tomato stakes. Russ had bought a rake with a wide rectangular head and thin metal tines, claiming it worked more efficiently. But I liked the old one with the triangular head and thicker tines. I wasn't after efficiency. There's something soothing in raking. The repetitive movement, the immediate gratification, the achievement in accumulation.

Leaves have drifted like snow into corners, on windshields, steps. Trapped, hard-to-get-to places, where a gust of wind will spin them into dervishes, and I let them be. I loved strolling my babies in the fall, loved the surprise of veering unexpectedly off the sidewalk because leaves lay so thickly that the concrete path was hidden. Whit would strain over the stroller seat belt to grab leaves caught in the wheel spokes, and cram them in his mouth, stems jutting from his lips like porcupine quills.

Whit.

A pickup with a trailer of lawn equipment passed. The sign on the cab boasted YARDS MOWED, SOWED, AND RESURRECTED.

Resurrected. People just have no idea.

~

I'd reached for a carrot stick in a plastic container beneath a drooping strand of miniature lights in the shape of grinning ghosts. The owners of 522 Liberty Ave-to-be obviously had young children impatient for Halloween, still two weeks away. Ebie had rummaged through boxes in our attic, looking for our Halloween-themed decorations.

"Meany Matheny cuts off her lights on Halloween so no one will come to her door," Whit once correctly observed. "She ought to dress up as a witch."

One December I'd asked her if I could snip some of her mahonia shrub berries, big and blue as grapes, to add to my wreath. "No," she'd answered. Year in, year out, Meany Matheny's Christmas wreath was a tough straw circle. I drew closer to a cluster of familiar faces eerily angled and shadowed by the candlelit, wall-less house.

"All the young people drink now is vodka and water," Jimmy Dillard said. "What happened to beer?"

On a sawhorse table, oriental noodles in brown sauce looked like worms in a bowl, like something you'd plunge your hands into at a Haunted House, blindfolded. One Halloween, Whit had peeled grapes and passed them off at the door as eyeballs.

"You get looped faster with vodka," Jane McDonald said, "that's why. And vodka mixes with anything."

I reached across a platter of fried chicken for the vodka. Dark liquid in a pitcher looked like ice tea but might have been grape juice. I poured some into a Styrofoam cup already imprinted with the new owners' address. Vodka mixes with anything.

"How's Phillip doing at State?" Beth Lewis had asked Jenna Donaldson. She was leaning against a wall-to-be. For a pantry, I decided, or one of those huge refrigerators. "Did he frat?" she asked.

"Is *frat* a verb?" Anne laughed.

"Yep," Jenna answered. "He's in the middle of hell week."

I drew the first wide swath through the leaves with the rake. Hell week. They had no idea what hell week is.

The blower screech died and the afternoon sounds were restored, noises I know intimately from my open bedroom window. The staggered accelerating of the mailman's jeep, then idling at the curb while he made his delivery. The louder grumble of the UPS and FedEx vans, the lurch of city trash trucks, the whispery glide of cars, the rhythmic *bumpa bumpa bumpa* bass of radios turned up full volume in teenagers' cars after school. Except for dead summer or dead winter, my windows stay open. Even during pollen season, when fine yellow powder coats the sills.

Tok came a noise from the side of the house. *Tok.* I looked around, noticed Mrs. Matheny's bedroom window wide open. She must be cleaning the glass pane that tilted inward; I've seen her do it. *Tok* came the noise again, and I placed it: our weight-sensitive bird feeder. A heavy jay or greedy starling landing on the bar closes the opening and seals access to food. Go away. You're unwelcome here. Go pick on something your size, like Mrs. Matheny's mahonia berries. You're too heavy for our party.

~

I'd lost social navigation skills; had forgotten the feints and back-and-forths of the social fray, the jabs and sexual innuendoes.

"Guess this is the closest I'll ever get again to a pair of studs," Sally Grainger joked. She was standing in the framework, a lumber jail, whose crosspieces bore flickering votive candles.

"What's it like being an empty nester?" Maria Davidson asked Tim Holland. "Is it *so* much fun? Do you and Carrie just run around with no clothes on all the time?"

"All the time," Tim repeated. "We had to get dressed just to come over here."

I straightened a torch stuck into an open pipe where the bar sink plumbing would eventually go, and wondered, has everyone been doing this, has everyone been saying these same things, has all this gone one without me—the pleasure, the laughter, the looseness and intimacy?

"Hey," Anne said, "you're not holding up your side of the social contract."

"Doing what?"

"Talking."

It had been a long time since I experienced that tidal wave of panic at a party when you want to go home. Must. Have to. *Right now.* This instant. Not since I was pregnant had I felt it: not anger, but desperation.

"Do what I do," Anne advised. "When I look around a party and know it's going to be a long night, I turn to the person standing next to me and say, 'Tell me your life story.'"

"It's not just youth that's wasted on the young," someone nearby said. "It's oxygen."

"Need anything?" Russ asked me.

"Another drink. Vodka and . . . tonic."

"Okay."

I touched his sweatered arm. "He had just . . . he'd just . . ."

But Russ leaned into a conversation across the buffet table, a knotted bunch discussing house sales, the rapid changes to Liberty Ave. "They've bought the Willis mansion."

"From mansion to McMansion."

"What did it go for?"

I tried to look interested. But I don't care what houses go for. I care that my son is gone forever.

"Beside us?" Russ asked Franklin. "Hadn't heard. Oh no, not a renter."

He had just memorized his social security number for college, I was going to say to Russ, and had another drink instead.

"Damn," Russ said. "Renters never stay long. Transients."

⁓

Mrs. Matheny's front door slammed, one sound I've never heard, never. She's too deliberate to slam.

Another sound was missing this fall, too: the sound of her scritching her own rake across her yard, doing battle with the leaves from my pin oak. In the realm of leaves, pin oaks are fine as needles. They slip through tines of a rake, have no bulk to form mounds, refuse to collect neatly at curbs. But when a gust seizes a pin oak branch, its slivers fall prettily and thickly as snow.

Mrs. Matheny didn't own a blower of any sort. Not a whining, gasoline-powered backpack, or dinkier electric hand-held, or wheeled fan designed for speedy, minimum-effort removal. I knew what she'd like: one of those huge suckers, small versions of the city curbside vacuums, noisy and thorough, that convert beautiful, pesky leaves to instant mulch fine as sawdust. Occasionally I'd see someone doing odd jobs for her, and the black-headed boy dragging an overflowing trash can to the curb was probably one of them. He stuffed the contents—a fabric piece, a beige bedspread, perhaps—more firmly into the can.

~

"How about those ubiquitous Lassiters?" Anne said. "They're at every party in town." She glanced dismissively at the ubiquitous Lassiters. "Thank God for the name tags. All these tiny-hiney yummy-mummys look alike." She tapped my right shoulder. "Where's your name tag? There're sticker-things near the beer cooler."

I hadn't seen a beer cooler because I was drinking vodka. And I didn't need a name tag because everyone knew who I was. I heard the sibilant esses—*"inconsolable . . . a shock," " . . . the one who lost a child."* Shushing whispers that were audible even against the music. *"She's the one . . . I heard he was . . . such a waste."*

"Is that her?" someone said loudly enough for me to hear. One of Anne's tiny-hiney yummy-mummys, new to the neighborhood. "I thought she was a recluse."

I found Russ scooping salsa on a corn chip. "Can we go home?"

"A little longer," he said.

You don't have to stay long to hear them say it, to see the shaking heads and averted eyes, to sense the awkward withdrawings or even the rude interest: What will the hermit do?

Russ handed me a dripping chip and said, "You get out of something what you put into it."

I have a mother, I'd thought, and had another vodka. What I don't have is my son. *Such a waste.* And such a mistake, coming here.

~

The boy tried to shove the heap of fabric deeper into the overflowing trash bin, then turned to study the telephone pole plastered with stapled notices. "Does anyone really believe these signs?" he said loudly. "'Earn dollar signs dollar signs at home in your spare time.'"

I looked at him from across my yard, my pile of leaves. He had curly hair, Whit's hair, resembled the cartoonish figure of Whit on the Windsor senior class caricatures a parent had mailed to me, a belated graduation present. "What were they thinking?" I'd asked Russ, "sending this to us?"

"They were probably thinking you'd rather have it than not have it. Don't be unreasonable."

"Lost pets I believe," the boy went on. "Have house numbers painted on curbs I believe. Call 1-800-4-BRAIDS I do not believe. Lose thirty pounds in thirty days I do not believe."

He must be one of those crazies that occasionally wander into our neighborhood. Or a "gypsy," one of a skilled, deceptively innocent band of strangers who, without breaking or entering, managed to steal from homes left unlocked while their owners innocently took walks or ran to the library, or . . . raked leaves. I ignored him and returned to raking, taking care not to snag the encroaching ivy vines. But despite my caution, something caught in the tines.

I'd left the party without Russ, and found my way home by the high, cold, bluish glow of the regulation streetlight Mrs. Matheny had installed in her back yard after her husband died; for safety, no doubt, to deter would-be robbers. She didn't seek our approval, but then, we don't speak. Russ had stored the terrace furniture cushions so I'd sat on the bare metal slats and tried to watch the moon, the stars, a plane passing overhead. Two doors down another neighbor had added a back room with a vaulted ceiling or cathedral ceiling or whatever the word is, and the triangular wedge of illumination was friendlier than the streetlamp's.

"Why did you leave?" Russ said, coming from the library door to the terrace. "Anne told me you'd used up your cuteness quota." He shook his head, amused. "That Anne. What are you doing out here?"

Acorns dropped around us. They rattled on the bricks and pinged against the grill lid and the wrought iron. Listening to Russ was like swimming through oil. Vodka does have a taste, after all, like metal in my mouth.

"Somebody bought it," Russ was saying, "and no wonder. It's a perfect tear-downer."

Tear-downer was a Winwood noun now, like *empty nester.* There are bungalows and cottages and ranches and colonials and now there are tear-downers. I gripped the chair handrails to make the spinning stop.

The silhouette of Russ's head tilted. "But the husband got sick, and they decided not to take it on. So they listed it with a Realtor, who sold it to New Dim."

I tried to listen. New Dimension was a competitor of Lucas Construction. But Russ's words sounded so distant, as though he were talking through a tunnel. Didn't he see? Didn't it bother him? I looked pleadingly at the pale blur of his face. *Russ! We can never be part of that kind of event again. Those people, with their private jokes and frames of reference I've somehow missed or forgotten or lost in ten weeks of grief, are behind and beyond us. Russ!* I tried to say. Beseeching.

"New Dimension will either sell the lot or build a house," Russ was saying, "whichever happens first. So for now they're renting, which is unfortunate for us."

The stars were out. It wasn't going to rain and the grass seed wasn't going to germinate and Whit wasn't coming back. I stood, began an unsteady path toward the back door. I'm afraid of new neighbors.

They come in and take down trees, bring all their construction debris—graders and hydraulic lifts and squares of shrink-wrapped bricks like impregnable fortresses.

"Rentals bring down property values," Russ went on. My foot hit the step. "No maintenance, no improvement. And this one's a single male, apparently. And young. Young single males are the worst kind of renters. A neighborhood's nightmare."

New neighbors bring Port-O-Lets and mud and fast-food trash and Dumpsters and—I stumbled on the riser, fell, scraping my knees and palms against the bricks.

Russ pivoted. "Are you drunk?"

Tears sprang to my eyes. "You never even talk about him, reflect—"

"Reflect or obsess?" He opened the tool shed for the cushions. "People handle grief in different ways, Laura."

My husband's voice was loud, vehement. Yes. There are stomping, angry, fist-shaking-at-the-fates-and-the-world storms of grief, and thick black mires of suffocating-and-floundering-and-not-caring-if-I-sink swamps of grief. His. Mine.

"Of course I'm grieving, I'm not heartless. But one of has to cope!" he said. "One of us can't be morbid every minute."

Tell me that it dogs you, Russ. Never leaves your thoughts. Tell me if it does. So I'll know I'm not so very alone. So alien and so removed from that regular life. Russ!

"You've just pulled up the drawbridge and closed ranks. You're not even trying, not even going through the motions. You're . . . *stunted!*"

"I'm not stunted. I'm grown. And Whit wasn't grown. He never will be." I wiped saliva from my mouth with the back of my hand. "Is there a time limit on sadness?"

"You *are* drunk. Go make yourself throw up or you'll feel like shit tomorrow."

But I *was* trying. Tomorrow, when I lifted my arms to the cabinet for a coffee mug I'd think, *Why am I so sore? What did I do?* And then I'd remember raking, the reason for the ache. Like Whit, the leftover pain—so much stronger, and longer—remains, reminds.

I stooped to dislodge the obstruction: a plastic army man. One of Whit's, embedded and eluding the blower all these years, now freed. And I tried, I did, but the plastic pointed rifle punctured my palm, and my heart, and my eyes closed and filled.

"This time of year you can always tell who the criminals are."

I opened my eyes. Wielding a long-handled pruner, he was striding toward the gulf of ivy that separated our yard from Mrs. Matheny's. Striding with that sharp tool toward me.

"The criminals are the cheaters with green grass thanks to computerized irrigation systems that come on at five a.m. when the drought police are fast asleep."

He looked at me with eyes so purely black the pupils were invisible. Eyes beneath a low forehead and brows that met like a furry caterpillar. Eyes that on another face, one less genial and encouraging, would seem menacing.

"They're probably the same people who'll hoard drinking water and batteries in a nuclear aftermath," he went on, plunging into ivy knee-high with robust health. He stopped before the spiky foliage of Mrs. Matheny's pampas grass. "This thing needs a haircut."

The fence ivy needs a haircut. Whit's words.

With a single motion he severed the feathery spears at the base, then hacked through the mustn't-be-touched mahonia trunk as well. It fell stiffly into the ivy. "I have an irrational hatred for pampas grass and mahonia. Also Bradford pear trees."

I fingered the tiny grooves in the toy soldier's uniform, surprised that he knew *mahonia*. And that he had an opinion about Bradford pears; the same opinion as me.

"All lined up in medians like spades on a playing card," he continued.

That's precisely what they looked like. Stylized, unnatural.

"And the first to go in ice storms," he said. "They split right down the middle." He picked up the broomy shoots of pampas and pointed them at me. "You're not an ugly American since your grass isn't green. Or maybe you just don't have an irrigation system."

A salesman with a new pitch, then. I dropped the rake, went around the house for the burlap leaf tarp, and hoped he'd find another victim. But he was still there when I returned, just watching.

"Raking is so therapeutic," he said. "Blowing is faster, but you can't think while you're blowing."

The comment was so true that I held the rake tightly to me and looked hard at him. He was slightly built beneath a T-shirt as ragged as any of Whit's. Even through my sunglass lenses he was pale-skinned for someone so black-headed, but for the distinct shaving shadow around his jaws.

"Wish I had some leaves to rake. But there aren't any in this yard."

"You will when the pin oaks fall." The sound of my own voice startled me.

He threw his head back, gazed up into the high branches.

"She hates my trees," I said.

"Who?"

"Mrs. Matheny."

"Why?"

"Because of their leaves."

"Oh," he nodded. "Another irrational hatred."

I smiled.

"Look," he said, "she has teeth."

A car passed, scattering leaves at the curb near the overflowing trash can sprouting material. *Slish.* "She didn't like my son even coming into her yard," I said.

"Pollyanna."

"Pardon?"

"The mean man in the big house with the prisms."

My grip loosened with fresh surprise. "Right."

Somewhere down the street the school bus ground to a halt, another familiar afternoon noise. I knew the sounds, even the wind chime clinking on the house two doors down, even the whistly wheeze from the squeeze bone the dog worried next door. Mrs. Matheny couldn't hear anything because season after season her windows stayed tightly shut. She was hermetically sealed, like bacon.

"Thank you," I heard a mother say to the bus driver. *Thank you for delivering my child home alive to me.* Ebie wasn't on the bus; she was staying after school for a project, collaboration on a biography.

"We have these things called 'families' this year,

with one person from every grade," she'd sighed. I'd read the handout describing the school's latest scheme promoting communication and unity. "Families meet on Fridays after lunch, and every family has a Friday Topic. Last week we were supposed to share something 'hard' about ourselves. Lisa Todd said, 'My dad's a drug addict.' Just like that, like she was proud."

I vaguely knew Mike Todd; knew that he'd had chronic shoulder problems that led to painkiller abuse and a detox program that had failed to cure him. But while Lisa's forthrightness amazed Ebie, I'd been amazed and saddened by a child's ability to reduce a misfortune to its simplest term, to its lowest—and cruelest—common denominator. I pictured Ebie in the circle, waiting for her turn. "What did you say about . . . us?" I'd asked her. *My brother's dead. My mother's paralyzed.*

She'd snapped the rings of her notebook shut, and said only, "I'm sick of my friends."

The boy interrupted my thoughts. Boy. Man. "I'm a leaf man myself."

Here it came, the sales pitch for his services. "Thank you, but I do my own yard work."

Like a mechanical Pied Piper, the ice cream truck inched down Liberty Ave, allowing ample time for any child within hearing to dart inside and beg for money. Just as Whit had done so many afternoons. By the time the white truck decal'd with fading stickers passed the boy and me, we'd heard its tinkled repetitive version of "Do Your Ears Hang Low" seven times.

"The real question is not do your ears hang low," he said, "but how he listens to that for hours on end."

I smiled again.

He lifted his feet, treaded out of the ivy on the other side of the fence. My side. "I've always thought ivy is just kudzu with a pedigree."

I stared at him. Exactly, again.

"You can't really *rake* leaves that fall onto ivy. You just . . . bat them toward you."

"Yes, I mean, no, right."

"And you," he said, "must be Laura Lucas."

Lor-a, he pronounced it, instead of *Lahrah*.

"The mailman either got lost or lazy." He took two envelopes from his jeans pocket and looked at them. "Domino's Pizza has a deal for you, and—" he flipped to the next letter, "Uncle Sam is looking for Russell Whitford Lucas, junior."

I put the tiny army man in my pocket and reached across the fence for the misdelivered mail.

"Did you dig up some treasure?" he asked.

"I didn't dig it up, I just—"

"Unleafed it."

I nodded.

"Your son's? Russell Whitford Lucas, junior's?"

It had to come, of course. I'd asked for it. I'd let

myself out of a protected area, strayed even momentarily from an isolation zone, and look what happened. My fault.

"Yes. Whit's."

Somewhere down the street a child yodeled a Woody Woodpecker call, and the cheerfully crazy imitation made my hands tremble. Daylight Saving would end this month, and early darkness would force children indoors and the ice cream truck would hibernate for the winter and my windows would close against morning chill and I would not be gutted by something as innocently wrenching as a child's Woody Woodpecker call.

"And where's Whit?" the boy went on. "Away at college? Eluding the Selective Service?"

Another pickup with a trailer eased itself down the street made narrow by leaf piles at the curb. The trailer was filled with riding and push mowers, a collection of rakes and blowers fastened to the iron mesh sides.

I watched it pass the overflowing trash can and suddenly recognized the fabric: Mrs. Matheny's bedroom curtains I'd watched open and close for a hundred days. This boy wasn't her odd-job man. This person in the ivy holding spears of pampas grass in one hand and clippers in the other was Russ's neighborhood nightmare, the young, single, male, transient renter. While I was watching falling leaves instead of Mrs. Matheny's house, he'd moved into it.

"'Landscape Management,'" he read the truck's sign aloud. "What a euphemism! Why don't they just say We Do Yards?" He tucked the pruners under his arm and looked expectantly at me, waiting for my euphemistic answer.

"Whit's dead."

He dropped the tool, and the ivy rustled and swallowed it.

"Three months ago," I said, and waited for usual murmurs of comfort, the genteel condolences.

He looked at me. "How do you stand it?"

Chapter Six

MOM WAS OUT IN THE FRONT YARD WITH HER RAKE WHEN I got off the bus. She's very big on trees and leaves, loves them. She has this, like, postcard book of nothing but pictures of trees with quotes underneath them. Whit gave it to her for Christmas. Mom loves the piano, too, made me take lessons starting in first grade and now I'm in sixth. My piano teacher looks like Barbie because she wears so much makeup and has swoopy blond hair, but she lets me play regular songs instead of junk no one's ever heard of, even for recitals. Mom and me do this thing where she requests songs when I practice. The only thing Whit ever requested was the "Mission Impossible" theme. Mom loves Whit, too. Loved, I guess, past tense. You can tell right away what Mom loves and doesn't love. She hates all the construction on Liberty Ave, but I think it's okay. Exciting, sometimes. It's something new, anyway. Something that doesn't have to do with Whit.

The first thing she'll ask me is how school was, but I'm not going to tell her about Lunch Bunch because it'll make her sad. It's totally dopey, but I go. If you're in sixth, seventh, or eighth grade and your parents are divorced, you get to go out to lunch once a month and—I don't know—*talk*. I go to this private school where nobody's a loser and everyone's supposed to be nice all the time. Like, we have a dress code so no one has better clothes or cooler tennis shoes than anyone else. Like, if you want to be in the play you get a part even if you can't talk louder than a whisper, and if you want to be on the soccer team you get to be, so nobody's feelings get hurt and so we never win. My school doesn't post an Honor Roll and doesn't give out first place ribbons on Field Day, and at the Spring Fling carnival last year we couldn't have a dunking booth because it was "demeaning to the teachers" that everyone wanted to dunk. At Whit's boarding school, all that was just tough. He told me all about it. People got nicknames like Zero because they had no personality, or Wedge because they were dumb and a wedge is the simplest tool known to man.

Mrs. Evans asked me if I'd like to come to Lunch Bunch because of Whit. Everything's Because of Whit. I'd rather have had a dress-down day or a homework pass, but I said yes because Mrs. Evans looked so hopeful and because Lunch Bunch always gets back late from wherever they go and gets to miss some class. And it's something new. Last month we went to a taco place and this month we had Chinese, but the main reason I went is that there's this new girl in my class who was signed up. Her name is Bett and she looks totally like a boy. She rides my bus, gets off down the hill before I do. Everyday she plops right down at the front of the bus where everyone knows only the older kids get to sit. They'll throw your books out the window in a minute but they leave Bett alone. I've been watching her. Mom watches, too, out the window. Of her room, not the bus. It's because she's sad. Because of Whit. I'm sad, too, but what I was for a long time was just *mad*.

"You're going to just burn him up?" I asked Mom and Dad.

"Cremation isn't burning someone up," Mom said.

"Then what is it?"

"It's only Whit's *body*," Dad said, and Mom put her hands on her stomach. My speech teacher says that's an *invisibility tactic* which is something I can't explain any better than my parents could explain being cremated, but I like the sound of. I do *not* like the sound of "cremation." Is it on a tray in a furnace or what?

"Was it because he looked so bad from the wreck?"

"Four people are using Whit's organs," Mom had tried. "He doesn't need his—"

"Eyes?" I said, but then Dad had to follow Mom upstairs.

Mom was raking, and talking to Meany Matheny's yard man. I'd rake, but the real money's in mowing. Whit made money that way during summers and vacations, and I don't know what we'll do now that he can't. Now that he's gone. We don't have a lawn team—"yard armies" Mom calls them— because that's something Mom *doesn't* love. She won't let me mow the grass yet—if it ever grows again—but I've asked for a hundred years to get my ears pierced, and last time she said, "Fine, whenever you go to the mall." Which was a scary answer, even though I want pierced ears, because Mom said yes so easy. Because I should have to beg.

When I got close enough to hear, she didn't ask me how school was. She and this guy were talking about something even duller: the weather.

". . . an L.A. day," he said. He was leaning against the fence, not working. Meany Matheny would have something to say about that, I bet.

"What?" Mom asked.

"Where it's seventy-five degrees day in, day out. Like today."

"Is it? You've lived there?"

"Never been there in my life. But it's supposed to

be year-round perfect, isn't it? Isn't that the attraction? You're comfortable no matter what you wear."

"But no seasons. I'd have to have seasons."

"Mom," I interrupted.

"Hi, Ebie."

"Ebie," the guy repeated. "As in heebie-jeebie?"

What a dork. "As in Elizabeth."

"You must be the piano player I've heard." He held his hand over the rickety split-rail to shake and said *his* name, which sounded like *Eh-yet*. "What?" I asked.

"Sorry. I'm used to my mother dropping the l's, and a syllable. It's *Elliot*. As in 'Pete's Dragon.' As in 'I'll Be Your Candle on the Water,'" he said, and grinned at me. "When both of our windows are open, I can hear you playing."

Well. Though I am totally too old for Disney, that's one of the piano pieces Mom likes. I'm doing bell choir at school, too, and already know the Italian directions: *crescendo, tempo, pianissimo*. One time I was showing off how I knew all the words and Whit said, "Are you in the retardundo?"

"Elliot's renting Mrs. Matheny's house," Mom said.

"Where'd Mrs. Matheny go?" I asked.

"She vanished," he said, "like Mary Poppins." He rubbed his chin. "She went to have a stumpectomy."

"What's that?"

Elliot looked very serious. "An operation to remove a stump from someone's ass."

I laughed real quick and looked down at the ground, which I expected Mom to fall on. She didn't even let Whit tell me to *shut up*. But she giggled instead, something I hadn't heard forever. Because, you know, of Whit.

"I'm a surgeon, and removing stumps is one of my specialties."

Mom went along with the joke. "You don't look old enough to have had years of medical school."

"I also do amputations. Limb removals."

"I see."

"You do?" His grin was wide. "You don't."

"Gross," I said.

"My patients don't complain. They're trees."

If *ass* didn't bother her, this'll do it. End of conversation. Anyone who isn't a friend of a tree isn't a friend of Mom's.

"I—" she started.

"—'think that I shall never see'... Right?" Elliot said.

I knew that poem. I'd die if I was a man and my first name was Joyce.

"... not your electric company whacker. Don't worry, I'm a *humane* tree surgeon. An arborist. I'm very partial to trees."

Mom's expression was suspicious.

"I'm a conscientious objector. I won't take down a tree that's living. Those days, I feed the chipper."

Mom was quiet, but then that's what she is a lot. Because of Whit. I miss Whit, too, mainly at night. Sometimes I go in his dark room when they think I'm doing homework and stare out his window at cars' taillights going down the hill toward the McCalls', and the little red dots getting smaller in the blackness make me sad. I can't explain it. A burning in my stomach like when I used to get homesick at sleepovers. During September Lunch Bunch, Mrs. Evans said, "Whit was away at school, gone so much of the year anyway, maybe it's not as hard for you," and I wanted to throw my taco at her.

"I have soccer practice, Mom."

"You're a soccer player?" Elliot asked. "What's your record?"

"Last year we were undefeated. This year we're . . . defeated." I dug change out of my pocket. "Here's leftover money from the field trip."

"You can keep it," Mom said.

"I don't save change cause you can't buy anything with little stuff."

"Wow," Elliot said, then pointed at the boxwoods. "Nice work on the shrub spooks."

Well, I liked that, because I worked a long time on my Halloween boxwood people. I stuffed paper into gloves and wedged different masks into the branches and draped the whole bushes with fake cobwebs so each one is a different, fat, ghosty-looking shrub person with hands. I have a Freddy Krueger mask, and an old man with no teeth and a warty chin mask, and a monster mask with eyeballs that hang down from the sockets to the lips mask.

"Wait a minute," Elliot said, and went inside Meany Matheny's house. He came out holding a mask. It was a greeny-white stretched-down triangle with perfect O eyes and a perfect O mouth. "Can you use this?"

"Aren't you going to use it for Halloween?" I asked him.

"I'm too old to trick-or-treat, but not too old to save change."

"How old are you?"

"Twenty-eight. How old are you?"

"Ten." I fixed the mask on the last boxwood nearest Meany Matheny's house, or rather Elliot's now. The whitish empty face jumped out of the dark green branches, and fit perfect above this fake arm that you're supposed to dangle out of a closed car trunk.

"The Scream," Mom said, what Dad calls a non sequitur.

I looked at her. "Mom, you're doing it again," and she stopped.

"Doing what?" Elliot asked.

"Jiggling her knees. She doesn't even know she's doing it. I'm trying to break her." Mom kind of shrugged, like she was embarrassed and apologizing.

"Nervous habit?" Elliot asked.

"Habit habit," Mom said.

She looked at me, and I knew she was thinking about my habit of touching my arms. We have a deal we didn't tell Dad, that I'll try not to pull or rub my arm hairs and she'll try to stop shaking her kneecaps, and all of a sudden I wanted to hurt her a little bit.

"Why are you wearing sunglasses?" I asked her in front of Elliot, because I know why she's wearing them. So no one can see how red her eyes are from crying.

"The glare," she lied.

Elliot looked at me a second, then brushed a finger under his nose the way people do when they're trying to tell you a booger's hanging out. I touched my nose to check and he laughed. "Know how you make a Kleenex dance?" he asked.

"Huh?"

"You put a little boogie in it."

Me and Mom both laughed, but he hadn't for-gotten my sunglasses meanness, and said, "I wear polarized sunglasses when I'm up top. They make the sky bluer and the leaves sharper."

"Up top?"

"In a tree. Like Bert on the London chimneys in *Mary Poppins*."

"You sure do know a lot about Disney movies for a grown-up."

"Ebie," Mom said. But jeez marie, she won't even let me rent PG-13s yet.

"I have a friend who has them all, that's why," he said. "Once I put my nose right into a big bunch of leaves that looked caught in the branches," he said. "It was a squirrel's nest. Know what baby squirrels look like? Rats."

I laughed, but Mom didn't. I could tell that she still thought Elliot was the enemy. A hatchet man.

He could tell, too, because he said, "Sometimes it's not just about taking trees down. Sometimes they need . . . fixing. I do the trim work, take out diseased or dangerous or dead branches, or the ones that keep sunlight from others and stunt their growth. I'm on your side," he told her. "You ought to come with me sometime, watch something *interesting*."

That reminded me. "Can I have someone come over?" I don't have people *come play* anymore. I have people *come over*. Bett doesn't know anything about Whit, and that'll be good. She'll act regular, not dopey. Bett. Elizabeth is her name, too, I bet.

"Okay," Mom said to me. "Okay," she said to Elliot.

Chapter Seven

WHIT WOULD HAVE LOVED THE CAR, A BROAD BLACK patrolman's car, used. The front seat was cluttered with junk mail and soda cans, a stray T-shirt and single sock, a mug, furled magazines. A litter of objects familiar as the contents of Whit's dorm room. But this was Elliot Hatcher; Elliot Hatcher putting the key in the ignition, Elliot Hatcher pushing earphones across the dash, not Whit. I looked at the inspection sticker adhesived in the windshield corner. A date in June was punched, and I thought, *He was alive then. He'll have been dead almost a year when the inspection expires.* "I should . . ." I began. *I should stay home with my window and my trees and my leaves and my solitude.*

When I didn't complete the sentence, Elliot flicked a dashboard switch. "My radio responds to human voices. Try it. Say, 'Get louder.'"

Feeling foolish, I said, "Get louder." A voice flared immediately from the speaker and I jumped, surprised.

"Told you so. Try again, speak up."

"Get louder," I said again, and again the announcer's voice blared forth. "That's amazing!"

He exploded with laughter. "Now press this ridge on the steering wheel."

I leaned across the seat and pressed the leathery bumps. The announcer promptly boomed from the speaker, and I laughed at my own gullibility.

"Don't get out much, do you?" Elliot chuckled.

Well, no. Not since July.

"You went where?" Russ asked.

Ebie frowned at the baked sweet potato on her plate. "Can we have ramen for supper sometime?"

"On a job with Elliot, at this old estate out in the country. Where have you eaten ramen?"

"If you forget your lunch at school they give you a package of ramen."

Even the drive out had been beautiful. If nature had conspired to effect the driest summer on record, she'd compensated by producing autumn colors almost unearthly in their beauty. The smallest shrubs—strip mall cottoneasters and miniature euonymus struggling to survive amid fast-food

SUSAN KELLY

wrappers and exhaust fumes—were brilliant roadside
flares. Trees glowed pink-gold and butterscotch,
oranges in hued degrees of persimmon, rust, flame.
Spindly in spring but splendid in fall, a gingko was a
dazzling treasure of lemony coins. As though
morning chill hadn't penetrated their borders,
maples still clung to their green, yielding only a red
fringe, or a single crimson'd branch.

"Sienna, henna, ochre, mustard," Elliot said. "The
color of merlot if you look at a fire through it."

A black-barked sugar maple was so fiercely
yellow that it seemed illuminated from within,
glowing with light brighter than sunlight itself. Trees
nondescript in summer shone with fuchsia fluores-
cence now; looked fatter, fuller in their autumn garb.
Young saplings offered a color burst against the blue
sky like a child's drawing of a candle flame, a
teardrop.

"Banyan, baobab, beech, birch," Elliot said.

"Ash, maple, laurel, pine."

"Sycamore, sweetgum, mimosa, maple. Peach,
apple, cherry, pear."

"Uncle," I'd laughed. "You win."

I passed Ebie the rolls. "Did you have ramen because
you forgot your lunch?"

"No, but Bett forgets hers all the time because
she's ADD."

"Wait a minute," Russ said. "One new person at a time. Where did you go with this Elliot? And to do what?"

Fifteen miles from town he'd driven into roadless woods at the foot of a sloping meadow. Far up the hill I glimpsed white clapboard of a large colonial home. Parked or wedged before us, or simply halted by undergrowth and trees, were ugly bulky vehicles: flatbed trailer, dump truck, chipper, stump grinder, front-end loader, forklift, slat-bed truck. "It's that hickory," Elliot said, and pointed through the car window.

Gold leaves fluttered down from the hickory's high branches. A six-foot volunteer magnolia hugged its trunk, and even the lowly no-name vine twining through the evergreen branches of the magnolia had been granted its moment of splendor. The glossy jade leaves that had hidden the vine all summer were no more than backdrop now to the red leaves bright as a strand of Christmas lights.

"The far side of the trunk is hollow halfway up," Elliot said. "Lightning, maybe. Or disease, insects. One big gust and the hickory will take four other trees down with it, so the owner wants it out. This is an easy job because we can be messy. In civilization, with yards and parks and streets—"

"Like Liberty Ave," I said.

"—like Liberty Ave, we have to be careful about where branches and sections fall. Careful not to crush a garden or a car or patio furniture. That's what I like about tree work. Every situation is different. Never the same day or the same tree twice."

Near the doomed hickory four men unloaded a blower, trash cans, chain saws, loppers, long-necked gas cans, an oversized wheelbarrow. "No ladders?" I asked.

"Ladders are for pruning. Can't use boot hooks for pruning."

"Because you'll kill the tree?"

"Wouldn't do it any good." Elliot smiled. "'You.' 'Kill.' All those personal, violent terms are giving me a complex." He'd opened the door and climbed out. "Come watch."

Russ forked his chicken breast. "What is this, paprika? Elliot who? "

"From next door," Ebie answered her father. "Hatcher. Get it? He hatchets trees."

"How did you meet him?"

"Raking," I answered my husband.

"This is Laura," Elliot said to the men stomping weeds and saplings at the base of the hickory tree. *Lora.* To a Latino who, even in his cowboy hat, was shorter than I. To a youth who looked no older than sixteen. To a stocky man in a lumberjack plaid, and a mustached, weather-beaten man in a long-sleeved T-shirt. Diego, Gus, Mack, and Flick nodded briefly, then turned to a tangle of leather and webbing and steel lying on the ground.

"This is the saddle," Elliot explained as he touched each one. "Choker, pulley, rope winch."

The carelessly strewn tools looked lethal as medieval torture instruments yet harmless as stable tack: coiled ropes gray and limp with use, webbed straps, cracked leather harnesses, pewter-hued steel hooks and spurs and winches and clips and pulleys. Nothing there seemed remotely akin to the fancy, lightweight, ultra-efficient, carefully maintained gear of mountain and rock climbers, but instead heavy and substantial and utilitarian, comfortably worn and old-fashioned.

The mustached man strapped on a hard hat and fastened himself round the waist to the hickory. He hoisted a leg, dug a spurred boot heel into the trunk and began the ascent.

"Why Flick?" I asked.

"Something to do with his hair," Elliot shrugged. "I don't know his last name. People come and go in the tree trade. For a lot of folks, that's the appeal."

Transient, I remembered Russ saying, and Whit—

"I only have four summers left before I have to go to work for the rest of my life," he'd said, biting off the tip of his dip cone as we stood in the Dairy Queen parking lot.

"Where did you get that idea?" When I was his age, the upcoming weekend was the only future I'd planned. "Go to Alaska for six months after you graduate, go to Wyoming for the next six months, then to the Keys. It's your life."

But my hand-to-mouth adventure-existence suggestions had no effect on him. "I'm scared."

I'd been touched by his simple confession made without sheepishness or sarcasm or apology. I admired his forethought, yet was struck with tenderness for his premature anxiety. "Everybody's scared then, Whit," I'd said. "Something will happen, a road will unfold. You have college ahead. So much fun, so many experiences. Don't worry about the future now."

Ten minutes later, Whit's future had ended. *I only have four summers left*, he'd said. No, not even that.

Carabiners jangled from Flick's leather belt alongside a handsaw and chainsaw that banged against his jeaned thigh. Shifting a rope lasso upward in a practiced, fluid motion, he scaled the broad trunk with a series of wide steps, hitching his legs. I imagined the strength of his thighs, to simply walk up a perpendicular tree trunk as if on a sidewalk stroll. He wore no work gloves, yet snapped off blocking boughs as he rose, and as they fell silently I pictured, too, how calloused those hands must be,

and looked automatically at Elliot's own hands, busily
tying knots in a length of rope. "Stationary bowline,"
he was saying, "clove hitch, taut line hitch."

Mack unclipped a walkie-talkie from his belt and
muttered something into it. "Flick forgot his walkie-
talkie when he went up the trunk," I said.

Elliot laughed. "Mack's talking to a crew at
another site, not Flick."

Higher, and twiggy branches became wrist-
thick. The chainsaw sputtered to life in Flick's hands
and Diego and Gus backed away as severed branches
dropped clumsily, leaving pale circles like fresh scars
on the hickory's trunk.

"He lops off lower branches to make room for
the weight bag."

"Weight bag?"

Elliot toed a long, pleated leather shape that
resembled a deflated rubber punch bag of my childhood that we banged against our wrists when it was
blown up. "Diego," he said, and as if it were understood shorthand, the Latino fastened a rubber length
to two neighboring tree trunks. "The world's largest
slingshot," Elliot explained, "to get the weight bag to
Flick and get the ropes into the trees."

"Why doesn't he just carry it?"

"A hundred feet of rope? Too heavy."

The bag shot upward, snagging on a branch eight
feet away from Flick. Unfazed, he used the handsaw

as a grabber to reach and draw it to him. Below, his co-workers talked and smoked, paying no attention to the methodical business of the man suspended sixty feet above them. Flick leaned back nearly at a right angle to the trunk to survey the tree's crown.

"How does he do that so smoothly?"

"It's like anything else, growing accustomed to something. The feel of the hooks, the strength of the branches, the heights, the weight of the saw in your hand."

Not grief, I thought. You don't grow accustomed to that.

Russ took a sip of water. "How old is this boy?" he asked. "What's he like?"

"He's not a *boy*, Dad, he's twenty-eight, I asked him," Ebie said, and turned to me. "Did you get to go up in one of those lifter things?"

"It's called a bucket," I said.

Russ eyed me with surprise.

"A bucket truck is used only for trees that won't support a man," Elliot had said. *May-un* he'd pronounced it, drawing the word into two lengthy syllables with a laugh and squaring his shoulders in apelike posture. I thought of Whit, flexing his arm on the pillow for my benefit.

Flick was now as small as an insect on a tapering

trunk stripped of everything but its leafy summit, a burst of gold foliage that looked like a sunflower against blue sky, or a toothpick's frilled cellophane topping. In a breeze unfelt at ground level, the hickory nonchalantly tossed its rippling leafy head like a debutante denied a dance. It seemed impossible that the denuded, swaying trunk could remain erect and vertical, blithely unaware of its fate.

"What's it like . . . up there on top of the world?"

Elliot hesitated, groping for an adequate description. "Lovely." I smiled at the feminine word coming from a masculine mouth. "Private. Peaceful. No noise but wind in leaves."

A warning whistle came from far above us, the chainsaw roared, and with a sickening *crack* the hickory's bushy crown fell earthward, the huge branch's downward plummet made both graceful and pathetic by the thousands of leaves slowing its descent and breaking the blow of its landing. Even grounded, the branches reached upward, ten feet high. A tree no longer a sunflower, or debutante, or even a capped toothpick. A tree now nothing more than a high stalk, an asparagus spear. I swallowed.

"Here's where the real skill comes into play: sectioning. How long the section is depends on the room below. Eight- or six- or four-foot lengths."

A line as thin as a spider's filament from my perspective sagged between the hickory and a neighboring tree. Flick leaned back, applied the saw's teeth to the trunk directly before him, and then chewed another partial cut into the trunk inches above the first. Golden motes of sawdust glinted, and the melon-shaped slice pitched down like a brick, bouncing into the undergrowth. Flick blew sawdust from the gaping wedge, checked the depth of his cut, and leaned his weight forward against the trunk, pushing. With perverted grace the section toppled, fell with a drooping swoop, and clunked against the tree trunk when the rope caught it, suspended above our heads.

Diego and Mack yelped with triumph, but what I heard was the brutish meaty sound of wood slamming into wood. "So a nearby tree is an unwitting accomplice in killing its neighbor."

"But now the neighbor has more room to breathe." Elliot slid off the car hood. "This is where I come in."

The undergrowth parted and a blond man held a sapling aside for the small towheaded child who followed him. Father and son, clearly. "I'm Allen Strickland," the man said and gestured to the big house above us, "from up the hill. How's it going? Will you be able to finish today?"

"Easy," Elliot said. He looked at the boy, dressed in army fatigues and a camouflage jacket. "And who are you?"

"Allen Theodore Strickland the third," he said. "I'm six. This is what I wore on Halloween."

"That's an awful big name for a soldier," Elliot said. "How 'bout I just call you Sarge?"

Allen Theodore Strickland the third beamed.

"Keep back, now," Elliot said, and joined Mack, Diego, and Gus in lowering the section to the ground. The knot was loosened and Flick drew up the rope length, winched himself four feet lower on the trunk, and tied a new knot. Again the jarring saw and jet of sawdust, again a cut crescent as pale as pumpkin flesh, again the gunshot crack and disturbing noise of wood slamming against wood, again the metallic chink as pulleys and winches and saws were adjusted.

Flick reared back against the safety belt, elaborately rotated his arms and shoulders, then removed his helmet and ruffled his hair. "Tarzan's showing off for you," Elliot laughed and, yodeling up him, stripped off his own T-shirt and waded into the leafy thicket of fallen branches. His bare shoulders were polished by sunlight pouring through a new hole in the forest where the hickory had been.

I inwardly squirmed, wondering if the crew thought I was Elliot's—what? Girlfriend? Right, at my age. Mother? Surely not, at my age. "I should have brought binoculars," I said.

"Bett's lived about a thousand places," Ebie said. "She's so cool.

Russ positioned his fork and knife across the lip of his empty plate. "Was it safe?" he asked warily.

"Aren't you afraid of—"

"Afraid of what?" Elliot asked me.

"Anything, everything. Crushing a hand when he leans against the section. Suppose it toppled the wrong way? The wedge could bounce off his toe, knock his boot hook loose, sawdust could spray in his eyes, a knot could slip, a—"

All the myriad opportunities for accidents. Missteps, miscuts, miscalculations. A section swinging backward could knock a human being off the trunk like nothing more than a pesky squirrel. A slipped finger could mean a severed arm or leg. A rope could tangle and tauten around an ankle, a neck. Afraid, simply, of falling, of tumbling through space in one careless moment of inattention. The earth wouldn't quiver, wouldn't tremble slightly as it did when a thousand-pound section of trunk slammed into it.

Elliot looked at me in a critical, interested way. "Can't you see the beauty in it?"

There *was* a beauty to it. A beauty in the process, the deliberate methodical pace, its unhurried precision and repetition. The ascent, the knotting, the slingshot, the circling of the trunk, the stabbing of

the boot heel, the drawing up of the line, the tightening. A beauty to the golden spume of sawdust like
flour sifted on our shoulders. A paradoxical beauty in
the puny vine whose leaves were already crimped
and wilting in death, unlike the springy, still-living
foliage on fallen boughs, unaware that the chipper's
steel-teethed jaws awaited. Beauty even in the small
mountain of leaf and bark mulch as fine and as deep
green as Christmas tree boughs in the rear of the
dump truck. A beauty like that of a smothering
snowstorm, a hurricane. And a beauty, yes, in the raw
physicality of it, man against mammoth.

"Yes," I answered Elliot, "very beautiful."

"Yes," I answered Russ. "very safe."

"So what was it like?" Ebie asked.

"It was . . ." How could I tell her? Like nothing I
expected, an eerie combination of balletic grace and
savage machinery, meticulousness and carelessness,
violence and tenderness, silence and noise, threat and
safety, tedium and attention. Dramatic yet purely
pedestrian. Five men, four hours, one tree. I smiled at
Ebie. "Like an assembly line. Like putting together a
television or car. And noisy!" My eardrums still
reverberated with the chainsaw's noisy scale: high
whine, low idling hum, steady monotoned drone,
comforting purr, *blat-blat-blat* bursts of trigger-happy
revving. So, too, the guttural groanings and pitched

screeches of chipper, the pounding of logs whose tonnage was impossible to calculate hoisted by the front-end loader onto the slat-sided truck. The soundtrack to Elliot's Forest Symphony, I thought, and reminded myself to tell him.

"Come on, Teddy," Mr. Strickland said to his son. "We've got a long walk back up the hill."

Teddy, I thought, and smiled. Like Russell Whitford Lucas, junior, the child was doomed to lifelong confusion about his middle name nickname. "Why'd you do that to me?" Whit had said. "Filling out forms is a nightmare."

"Can I come again?" Teddy asked Elliot.

"Talk to your dad about that, Sarge. He'll have to find us some more trees."

"We have *tons* of them!" the child assured Elliot and put his hand into his father's.

"Elliot says your name funny," Ebie said.

Russ peered at me again, swept spilled salt into his palm. "Take your plate to the counter if you're finished, Ebie."

"Glad you came?" Elliot asked on our way back to town. I pulled down the visor and a sleeve of CDs dropped into my lap. For my Christmas present Whit had burned a half-dozen CDs for me. But I hadn't touched the discs since July, too aware that the sight of the familiar cramped slant of his handwriting ("I've been practicing my signature, Mom.") on the silver surfaces would blur my vision for the rest of the day. Listening to songs he'd specifically selected for me—picturing him at the computer, grinning as he clicked and downloaded—was out of the question. **OLD SOUL**, he'd titled one, and **A REEL VARIETY** of instrumental movie themes. **PARROTHEAD** I'd broken in half and deliberately placed in the kitchen trashcan beneath coffee grounds and cantaloupe rinds. I looked out the car window, away from a slotted CD labeled **EXPLICIT**.

"Something's going on up ahead," Elliot commented.

Though the intersection light was green, we were held up by an impromptu parade of slow-moving, gaudily decorated cars, soaped with exclamation points and stars and slogans. GO PIRATES! WE'RE NUMBER #1! BEAT THE BENGALS! Red and white crepe paper fluttered from antennas and bumpers and door handles. Laughing teenagers with painted faces hung from open windows, waving their arms, shouting and singing, oblivious to delayed and irritated grown-ups, and to the sudden lurch in my gut as I watched their delirious enthusiasm. The pangs of pain. Another landmine.

"It's the final football game of the season

tonight," I answered Elliot, "at Page High." They honked and hollered, chanted cheers and jeers, grabbed at one another from open windows, yelled to friends in other cars; all motion and laughter and enthusiasm on their way home from the pep rally. They hadn't a care in the world beyond the immediacy of this glorious, blue-skied, late fall afternoon, beyond this excitement and anticipation, this joy in each other. Beyond sheer, pure, unadulterated euphoria, and the powerful certainty that this moment is absolutely perfect.

"Duck!"

Jolted aware, I realized we'd reached Liberty Ave. Elliot pulled up behind a construction Dumpster the size of an army tank, then reached across the seat and yanked on my shirt. "Mormons! Hit the floor!"

Straddling bicycles, two white-shirted, black-necktied youths were solemnly consulting a sheaf of papers in the street in front of Elliot's house. He contorted his frame beneath the steering wheel, laughing. "Hide!" he whispered fiercely, and I obeyed, giggling as I slipped down to the floor mat. For long minutes we held our breath, shaking with suppressed mirth at our deviousness.

"Oh, have a heart, they're required to be missionaries. We have to be scratched off their list of Must Accomplish," I whispered.

"How do you know, were you one in a former

life? Sshh," he commanded, and then cautiously raised his head to check on the Latter-day Saints' whereabouts, cursing when he banged his shoulder on the steering wheel. "Ollie ollie oxen free."

I laughed. "Aren't you interested in Joseph Smith?"

"And not in who my ancestors are, either," Elliot said.

"Do you know anything about this . . . Elliot?" Russ asked. "Beside the fact that he's a tree man?"

I turned on the faucet. "Arborist."

You're not sad, Elliot had said, *you're just optimism-impaired.*

Russ put the butter dish in the refrigerator and smiled at me. "Fraternizing with the enemy. Did it confirm all your worst opinions about tree people?"

Lemon fragrance rose from the sink of suds and I remembered the day's smells of machinery and human sweat and raw lumber. And of earth too, its aroma released when the jagged sawed edges of falling trunks gouged huge divots. "'I like trees because they seem more resigned to the way they have to live than other things do,'" Elliot had said. "Willa Cather."

I leaned to put forks in the dishwasher basket. "It was—"

"I spent my day at a site," Russ interrupted, and hoisted his shoe to his knee, checking for dirt.

A relief is what it was. A relief to forget my grief.

Russ leaned forward and ran his hands down my back, tracing my spine. "I'm glad you . . . *did* something today, Laura. That you . . . went out. Let's have him over. I'd like to meet this Elliot."

This Elliot. "Alright."

Chapter Eight

"Let me do Thanksgiving," Anne said. We rotated Thanksgiving Day lunch annually between our house and the McCalls'.

"No," I said, "it's our year, and I want to." *I am resuming.*

"What can I bring, then?"

"A sweet potato casserole? Green beans?"

"Fine. Oh, and Dixon's going to Memphis with a friend, so don't count him in. This will be the first time we haven't been all together at Thanksgiving."

Only three of us, too. No Whit. Wonderful, thoughtless, forgivable Anne. "Yes."

"Bett and her mother get to go to a restaurant for Thanksgiving," Ebie said when she heard the plan.

Russ was changing the light bulb I'd neglected for so long. "'Get to'?" he said. "Maybe they have to. Where is this child's father, anyway?"

From the floor of the closet Ebie said, "Grown-ups think Thanksgiving is the best holiday of the year." She twirled a tassel on her father's loafer. "But it's the boringest."

"Because Thanksgiving is calm," Russ said, gently shaking free of her fingers. "It's not about *getting*; it's about getting *together*." He was pleased with my decision. Normalcy. Progress.

And it was a kind of pleasure to plan and prepare; carving candle ends to fit holders, changing oven racks to accommodate the turkey, scouring cookbooks for a better dressing recipe, polishing never-used silver goblets, dusting the little-used dining room, counting napkins, arranging squash and pomegranates and lady apples and walnuts to spill from the wicker cornucopia centerpiece.

"Do I have to wear a dress?" Ebie asked.

"Sure," Russ answered, "why should this year be any different?"

Just a little different. "I never brought food when you moved in," I'd told Elliot when I'd invited him, and at his quizzical expression added, "That's what people do for newcomers and sickness and . . . deaths. Come."

Darrell held open the kitchen door for his wife and daughter, then kissed me on the cheek and said softly, "Happy Thanksgiving." Russ's partner of fifteen years was different from Anne in a good way; their contrasts served their marriage well. He was the foil for her directness and penchant for hyperbole. Darrell was calm, self-contained. Like Thanksgiving. "What?" he said, noticing my smile.

"I was thinking how you're like Thanksgiving." Nonplussed, he gave my shoulder an encouraging squeeze.

"Is there room in the oven?" Anne asked, removing plastic film from a casserole. "This needs to be warmed."

I turned to Adele, my godchild, whom I hadn't seen in the months since she'd gone to college and I'd gone inside to shut out everything but my despair. Though Adele knew my kitchen as well as she knew her own, she hung back, as uneasy with her role today—and perhaps with her feelings—as she'd been at Whit's funeral. Even through the haze of grief and ritual, I'd noticed Adele's distress, unsure whether she should consider herself family or girlfriend or both. She'd been Whit's childhood playmate racing Big Wheels down the sidewalk and later, bicycles down Liberty Ave. She was his fellow explorer in the Deep Woods, the other half of a duo in neighborhood games and industries and conspiracies.

"Fine godmother I've been," I told her now. "I didn't make you any Kool-Aid." She and Whit would come indoors clamoring for the sweet fruity pop Anne didn't allow at her house. I kept a dozen of the packets for Adele to mix a pitcherful, scooping far more than the single cup of sugar suggested by the directions. "Are you still a Kool-Aid fanatic or would you rather have a Bloody Mary?"

Adele smiled then, white teeth in a pretty heart-shaped face still faintly tan from summer or the Florida sun, where she was in college.

When Whit went away to boarding school, absence and puberty altered the pair's perspective and emotions and, eventually, their relationship. Whit welcomed Adele's obvious crush on him, grateful not only for the attention but that she kept him connected to Greensboro friends during vacations.

"Only a virgin Mary," Anne answered for her daughter.

I winked at Adele and remembered the afternoon Anne and I took a walk not long after Whit's return to Windsor after spring break of his junior year. Near the park, where we chased cars from the tree roots, a pair of limp tights lay discarded on the street. "I hope those didn't come out of Adele's car," Anne had said, and though we'd laughed and walked on, I'd had a sudden clench of concern about the extent of our children's intimacy.

I pushed a drape of brown hair behind Adele's shoulder. "How's Rollins?"

"Good," she said. "Fun."

"She's learning about laundry in Independence 101," Anne said. "That washing blue jeans with lingerie equals gray bras. When I answer the phone she wants to know about bleach, or boiling eggs. Unless it's a two in the morning call, crying."

"What?" I asked. "Why?" Crying about Whit?

Adele blushed. "It's so noisy, all hours. People coming and going, music playing, doors slamming. Sometimes I can't get to sleep, and I get . . . panicky, that I'll be so tired the next day I can't function."

"Adele's roommate went to boarding school, so she can sleep through anything." Anne suddenly halted in her crouch before a low cabinet. "Oh Laura, I'm sorry. I just didn't . . . think."

"Do we have any lemon pepper?" Russ called from the den.

"Are you going to send me away to school?" Ebie asked.

I pulled the rubber band from a bunch of celery. *We could have had those years with Whit*, Russ had said, *if he hadn't been away at school. If you hadn't*—he'd said, stopping just short of accusation.

Don't. Don't do that to me. You wanted it, too. The safety of it, the wholesomeness. The experience and the exposure and the education. You did, too, Russ, you did!

Only because you did. I would have kept him at home. Maybe this had been a mistake. Maybe we should have gone to a restaurant for Thanksgiving lunch after all.

"What did you say, Ebie?" Russ asked, coming into the kitchen.

"Ebie," Anne said swiftly, "come show me where your mother keeps the serving spoons."

"I'll cut the celery for the Bloody Marys," Adele said.

"Lemon pepper is on the spice rack," I told my husband.

"Everything looks so pretty," Anne called from the dining room. "Have you always had these organdy placemats? But—" She came to the swinging door. "Oh, Laura," she said softly. "You forgot, and set seven places. I'll take off the extra."

"Anne," I said, equally softly. "You don't *forget*. I invited someone."

Her face relaxed with interest. "Taking in strays? Who?"

"Laura's gotten herself involved with a tree hugger named Hatcher," Russ said. "And how's this for an oxymoron? He cuts them down."

Stray? Involved? They weren't the words I'd have chosen. "Our next-door neighbor," I began, "he has to work on Friday and can't go home so I—"

The doorbell rang and Ebie sprinted to open it. "No one uses the front door!" she said delightedly to Elliot.

He stood in the doorway wearing a checkered shirt and jeans and holding a six-pack of beer. "I knew I should bring something," he said, "but this was the only thing I could think of. It was also the only thing in my refrigerator."

"See," Ebie complained, "*Elliot* didn't dress up."

His jeans, his beer, his sheepish grin, his easy-going humor, were at once relief and encouragement for me. "It's fine," I said, thinking, *and now lunch will be fine, too.* I'd invited him out of kindness, yet now that he'd arrived it seemed the tables had turned: Elliot's presence was more favor to me than vice versa. "This is Adele McCall, the daughter of Russ's business partner."

"Did Page win its last football game?" Elliot asked her.

Adele started. "I don't go to Page anymore, but . . . they did, actually. How did you know about the game?"

Elliot shot me a glance, and I remembered the carloads of giddy teenagers whose infectious, unbridled exuberance had saddened me. "'Cause," he said, "I was young once, too."

Adele laughed at both his elaborate know-everything shrug and the suggestion that the one person in the house closest to her age wasn't young.

"I'm Russ Lucas," Russ said, joining us. "Welcome to our home."

Russ's formality embarrassed me, but Ebie dragged Elliot possessively toward the den. As I put ice in goblets, whisked gravy, I listened from the kitchen as the Macy's parade emcees listed the hometowns of bands playing "Hello, Dolly" and "People."

"There's the Pillsbury Doughboy float," Elliot said. "Looks like one of your boxwood people, doesn't it? Fat thing with big hands and head."

"It does!" Ebie said, thrilled with his Halloween reference, with his attention in an otherwise grown-up gathering. "I have your screamer mask upstairs."

"We didn't have as many trick-or-treaters this year," Anne said. "Normally cars full of children come from other neighborhoods."

I passed a tray of cheese and crackers. "Probably because there's nowhere to park between the construction Port-O-Lets."

"It's a good neighborhood," Russ reminded me. "That's why people are making improvements. Fewer trick-or-treaters means less vandalism anyway."

"It's finally dawned on me that the people who live in the house with the trampoline take their hammock inside every night so it won't be stolen," Anne said. "I hear the gypsies are back, so watch your unlocked doors."

Elliot wandered over to the bookshelf. "Lunch will be ready in a minute," I said. "Cheese cracker?"

He took one absentmindedly and pointed to one of the framed pictures. "Is that Whit?"

He said his name. He said his name without hesitation, without hushed tone. Until you've lived with averted eyes, until you've come to expect and dread the pauses, the avoidances of mention in a grocery store line, you can't appreciate the blessed normalcy of an everyday question holding nothing more than curiosity and interest.

I looked at my boy. Wearing shin guards and clutching a hockey stick, he was bent over in concentration during a pickup game at the park, oblivious to the newspaper photographer. A monster pink bubble ballooned from his mouth. "He was eleven."

"Bet he hated that headful," Elliot said, and I knew what he meant: the lush curls, a tangled mop of uncomb-able, uncontrollable ringlets.

My fingers went weak and I set down the tray on the cabinet shelf and steadied myself against it. "Yes. He did."

"I hated mine when I was eleven." He clamped his hand over his own headful of curls. "Because sixth-grade girls loved boys who had bowl-cut, straight-down bangs."

Oh, yes.

"But our kind of hair doesn't grow *down*, it grows *out*. My mother called me cherub head, and my classmates shortened it to shrub head. And on some days, Mushroom."

I wiped dust from a frame I hadn't touched in four months. "Whit's nickname at Windsor was Nuke."

"For nuclear hair," Elliot said.

Exactly.

Ebie reached between us for a cracker. "Whit got the good hair," she said, cruising on. "I want corn rows."

"And is this you?" Elliot asked.

I looked at a picture Anne had taken. Ebie was a pink blanketed blob in a stroller seat and I sported a set of winged bangs. "I keep that picture to remind myself of when I was younger," I said.

"I thought maybe you kept it as a reminder never to cut bangs again," he said.

Surprise and shock made me laugh. Surprise at his candor, because I *did* look awful with bangs, just awful. And shock at . . . what? An unexpected flood of warm affection for Elliot; a frisson of pleasure in his observation, an appreciation for the implied compliment that I looked better now, that he'd looked closely enough to notice a difference in my appearance.

"Laura?" Russ said when my laughter rang out in the room. "Are we ready?"

Not until I filled my plate, last in line at the sideboard, did I turn and realize I'd assigned no places at the table. Anne and Darrell and Adele and even Ebie stood awkwardly and anxiously by, confronting this new landmine—who will sit in Whit's vacant chair?—and waited for direction from the hostess. Me.

And then Elliot simply put his plate on the table and innocently sat down in Whit's lifelong place. "Oh boy," he grinned, "all my favorite food."

I can do this, I thought. *I can.*

Anne picked up a delicate salt cellar of curved blown glass. "This is beautiful."

"My artsy Aunt Ag gave it to me for a wedding present. I've finally grown to appreciate it."

Anne reached for the matching pepper. "How can you remember that?"

"I don't know. I can walk around the house and still name who gave me those bookends for a wedding present, who gave me that rooster vase. After nineteen years I can still reel off my OB's phone number."

"Eleven years," Russ said. Forks clinked in a sudden uncomfortable silence.

Elliot took a sip of water. "I love the way cold silver feels against my teeth."

Darrell rose. "I'll uncork the wine."

"And where did you grow up, Elliot?" Russ asked. The avuncular tone, the suggestion that Elliot was a child to be condescended to, irked me. I purposely filled Elliot's wine glass first.

"In the shadow of an army base," he replied

cheerfully. "Fayetteville. The most important day of the week was payday Friday and the most important store was the pawn shop. Listen." He growled deep in his throat, a wicked, perfect imitation of a blatting, revving motorcycle. Anne and Darrell laughed and I thought of the camouflage jacket Whit had purchased from the army surplus store while I'd thumbed through pamphlets with alarming titles and instructions for creating homemade explosives and ways to avenge yourself on annoying neighbors. I smiled inwardly, thinking how that information could be handy these days to chase off Liberty Ave invaders with their construction permits.

"My mother still speaks fondly of Jeffrey McDonald," Elliot was saying. "She wrote him in prison."

"That man who murdered his family and claimed hippies did it?" Anne asked.

"But he was *framed*!" Elliot grinned. "Or so his hometown supporters believe."

"I don't know how anyone could believe that roving-hippies story," Russ said. "There wasn't a shred of evidence. What a hoax."

"So was the moon landing," Ebie said, "a hoax."

"What?" Russ asked.

"Bett told me. They didn't really land on the moon or walk on it or anything. The whole thing was a video."

"Ebie—" Russ began.

"Bett knows all about it." Ebie ticked off the reasons on her fingers. "There was no exhaust from the space ship. Those astronauts couldn't get through this thing called the Van Allen Belt without dying of radiation sickness. The flag moves but there's no wind in space. And those heavy steps on the moon aren't real, it's just regular walking taped in slow motion."

Darrell sat back, listening to Ebie's impassioned logic. He'd been quiet, even for Darrell, and I wondered at the reason.

"The crosshair in the camera is covered up. Plus there are two sources of light, two shadows, and there's only one sun in our solar system, right? What they did was just film it in Area 51—"

"What's Area 51?" Elliot asked

"Some desert out west that looks like a moonscape. When the rocket went up, all the astronauts really did was orbit around for a while and then come back to earth." Ebie looked around with satisfaction and waited for agreement.

"You know," Elliot began, "it's believable—"

"Who is this you're talking about?" Russ asked.

"My new friend Bett," Ebie said impatiently. "I *told* you about her, Dad."

Russ looked across the table at me. "Do you know her?"

I shook my head no. "She and her mother are

renting the little metal house down at your end of the street," I explained to Anne and Darrell.

"Yeah," Ebie said. "Their whole house came from Sears! Isn't that cool?"

"I know who you're talking about," Anne said, and pushed rice to the center of her plate. "That's the oddest-looking child I've ever seen. Her forehead is black."

"'Cause she dyed her hair for Halloween and it hasn't worn off," Ebie explained.

Russ's expression was a mixture of dismay and perplexity. Elliot, though, was interested. "What was she?" he asked, "A gorilla? A witch?"

I laughed.

"I'll tell you what she is," Anne said. "N-o-k-d. Not our kind, dear."

"Anne," Darrell softly scolded.

"There's already a Christmas wreath up. Plastic. And a string of lights around a single window, like some country house out on the highway."

Anne's derision was lost on Ebie. "That's Bett's room. She decorated it herself. The lights look so good 'cause she has a mirror bead curtain since there isn't a door to her room, and a disco ball that she hung from the ceiling with dental floss."

"Never thought of dental floss," Elliot said. "Good as duct tape for what needs doing."

"Whit used duct tape for everything," I said.

Russ's hand paused on its way to his wine goblet. I'd done it again: made a hole in the conversation trying to fill the hole where Whit was.

Darrell smiled at me, then at Ebie. "Your friend Bett sounds like a cross between Eloise and *MAD* magazine."

"She's an only child. Like me."

When you have a cold, your eyes squeeze shut of their own volition. It's difficult to open them. I wasn't ill, but mine did. When I got them open, I was staring at the napkin in my lap, and Anne was talking.

"Speaking of our end of Liberty Ave, have you noticed those trees tagged with pink ribbons? The Lindsays—isn't that their name, Darrell? The yuppies who added on to the Dutch colonial?—have bought that adjacent ranch house for their addition."

"That's not an addition," Darrell said dryly. "That's an annex. The lot is completely overbuilt. The sidewalk setback is barely ten feet. Bigger, better, uglier is the new MO."

"How did they make their money?" Russ asked.

"Inherited a Budweiser distributorship, I think," Anne said.

But I hardly heard. "I thought the pink ribbons meant those trees were to be saved."

Russ spoke right over me. "Location, location, location, and we're sitting right on it."

Darrell shook his head. "Someone recently said

to me in all seriousness that it's very important to a neighborhood that school standardized test scores are good because prospective buyers believe houses will still have value in ten years."

I pleated my napkin, tried to compute this. Who made decisions along such lines? The rationale was crazy, the implication immoral. "What next, requiring children's IQs in addition to termite inspections?"

"The brick baby Monticello is up for sale," Anne said.

"Oh, no," I said. "I've always loved that house. Where are the Owens going?"

"They were never happy here," Russ said.

"How do you know?"

He chased a slippery pickled peach around his plate. "The house is so chopped up."

"Buck and Sandra Pinkard's house is on the market, too. They're separating," Anne said.

"That's a rumor," Darrell said.

"*Part* rumor. They're not separating, but the house *is* on the market," Russ said. "They just want to see what it's worth. Or what the piece of dirt it's sitting on is worth."

"Greedy, greedy," I said. Though the topic excluded Elliot, it was too important to me to end. "I could stand it if the tear-down replacements had any charm, but they're gee-gawed with scallops and sky-lights and pilasters. Everybody's got to have a turret."

"And columns," Anne said, laughing. *Colyums*, she derogatorily pronounced it.

"Ostentatious," Darrell agreed.

"Anyone for seconds?" Russ said, pushing his chair back.

I was bothered that my friends' and husband's observations seemed only that—observations, not opinions. "Don't you detest what's happening?" I asked the table. "Have you read those letters to the editor in the paper about this very neighborhood?"

"I read the one from Peter Carlson that said his property values went up every time a D. H. Griffin wrecking truck drove down the street," Russ said.

"I feel like—" I struggled, "like—"

"Mike Mulligan," Elliot said.

"Who?" Russ asked.

"No, not Mike Mulligan," Elliot corrected himself. He put a fist to his forehead, thinking. "The other story, where the skyscrapers are going up all around a house on a hill . . ."

Three pair of adult eyes gazed at him as though he were speaking Sanskrit. Not me. "*The Little House*," I said. "That's the name of the book. By Virginia Lee Burton."

"Exactly!" Elliot said.

"And that's exactly how I feel. It's disgusting."

Heads looked down at cleared plates in the silence. I'd done it again: screeched the dialogue to a halt.

"Say, Ebie," Elliot said, "have you ever had a serious operation?"

Ebie beamed. Elliot had done it again, too: saved me, saved us.

"Well," Darrell said, smiling and standing. "It's nice having Laura be passionate about something again. Who wants dessert?"

"Scram," Anne said. "Nobody can load more in a dishwasher than me. And don't look. No rinse patrols."

Everyone had helped clear, and with Anne commandeering the kitchen, little was left to be done. When Russ and Darrell wandered toward television and football, Adele left for a Thanksgiving Day tag football game with Greensboro friends she hadn't seen all fall. I'd walked her to the door and she'd suddenly turned and gripped my arms and pressed her smooth young cheek to mine. "I miss Whit so much," she whispered, and was down the front walk before I'd registered the sad fierceness of her confidence, as though her loss were a secret. The suncatcher dangling from her rear view mirror swayed as she drove away.

Voices reached me from upstairs, where Ebie had taken Elliot in search of the Scream mask. I climbed to the landing, eye level with the open door to Whit's room.

"... need to start babysitting," Ebie was explaining

to Elliot, "because Whit isn't here to pay me for favors anymore."

I leaned against the wall, not intending to eavesdrop over a cheering stadium crowd in the den, running water in the kitchen, but helpless not to. Helpless not to want to hear his name, spoken in the offhand, griefless voice of a child.

"What kind of favors?" Elliot asked her.

"Sending me downstairs to get his laundry when it's done, getting a CD he left in the car, addressing envelopes, you know."

She hasn't said these things to me. And though I long for just these details, I understand why. When the loss is so immense, trivia seems only that: trivial. Not significant, not important enough to be spoken of lest you be viewed as insufficiently serious or sad. I climbed to the upstairs hallway. Yet the small moments—the tiniest, most minute and ludicrous memories—are what you cherish most.

Ebie saw me. "Do you know where Elliot's screamer mask is?"

"I know where *I* stash everything," Elliot said. He knelt, lifted the dust ruffle, and his arms disappeared beneath the bed. "Candy wrappers, markers, pennies, a notebook and—" he ducked and peered—"oh boy."

"Did you find it?"

"Something better." He pulled out a flat box, put it on the bed, lifted the battered cardboard lid and grinned like a pirate with new-found treasure. "Crossfire."

It was Whit's toy, a game I hadn't seen, or rather *heard* in years. Elliot was already positioning the board in the middle of the bed, loading the plastic pistol with silver ball bearings. Ebie stooped to load the opposing gun attached to the board's edge, and in seconds they were at it, shooting the metal marbles across the playing board, trying to maneuver the small puck into the goal, and score. Any talent involved in aiming or strategy was lost, abandoned for speed in reloading and refiring.

"Loser!" Elliot whooped as the black disc dropped into Ebie's trough.

"Again," Ebie demanded, barely pausing, scooping a handful of balls into her pistol. Within seconds she'd lost again, and sat back, frowning.

Elliot pumped his arm in victory. "Two out of three, out." He looked up at me. "Next?"

It was irresistible. I hiked up my skirt, knelt beside the bed.

"Go!" Elliot shouted and we were off, zinging a dozen metal balls in rapid-fire succession back and forth across the board. Their rattle and roll across the cardboard, the clicking of the pistol triggers, the pinging of the marbles, all made for a noisy racket. But not as much racket as our laughter and our shouting.

"Mine! Those were mine!"

"You cheater!"

"No fair, you have more balls than me!"

"Wait, where's the puck? You *hid* it!"

It was hilarious, the goal of the game forgotten as we recklessly scooped and loaded and fired, our shoulders shaking with laughter and bodies writhing, contorted with giving it English, giving Whit's childhood game everything we had even as our fingers grew weak with repetitive motion, with hilarity, as we grabbed at the same flying, rolling balls, knocking one another's hands away, a couple of maniacs on the loose, until I fell backward on the thin slice of rug between the twin beds, ceding victory as I shook with the delicious helplessness of hysteria, too drained to even sit up.

"What are you doing?" I heard Russ ask from somewhere.

Hiccupping and chuckling, I dragged myself to my elbows, high enough to glimpse Elliot's open grin across the bed. He was beaming at Anne and Darrell and Russ, who stood in the doorway wearing expressions of amazement, disbelief, and bewilderment. Russ's raised eyebrows seemed to say *She has finally lost her mind after all.* I felt like a child caught pouring the entire box of bubble bath into the tub, and it felt wonderful. I wanted the bubbles to spill over the sides. I wanted them up to my chin.

"Playing Crossfire," Elliot said, innocence itself. "Want to play?"

"I do," Ebie said a sulky frown on her face. "But Mom's hogging you."

Elliot clattered balls into his pistol slot and as she stalked off, called out to her, "Do you need a nap?"

I stood, looked down at his curly hair, the loops of soft wool. "I say that to Whit. Said, I mean."

"You did?" he asked. "So did my mother."

His mother. I smoothed my skirt. Elliot was a child. And I'd been acting like one.

Russ gave me an unreadable glance and went in search of Ebie. "We ought to be going," Darrell said. It struck me again, how quiet he'd been. "Thanks for everything, Laura. Happy Thanksgiving."

Glasses tinkled as Russ lined them on the cabinet shelves. It was after ten, and we were putting up the last of the clean dishes. "Darrell seemed quiet today," I said.

"How could you tell between all the uncomfortable pauses?" Russ said.

"It's store-bought," Anne said, passing the thick maroon cylinder of cranberry jelly. "I remembered that Ebie likes it straight from the can, with the ridges still on it."

"I don't like cranberry jelly at all," Ebie said. "That was Whit."

"Maybe Darrell seemed quiet because Elliot dominated the conversation," Russ added.

I spilled silverware from the dishwasher basket to the counter. It wasn't fair and it wasn't true but I let the comment pass. "Darrell didn't even seem particularly glad about the Kirkwood contract, and you've been after that for months, haven't you?"

"Where does this pie plate go?" Russ asked, ignoring my question. We were pursuing different topics on a two-track conversation. "What do you know about Elliot Hatcher?"

The switch in subject caught me off guard. "I know he remembers *Mike Mulligan's Steam Shovel*."

"Is that it?" Russ asked.

I know he makes me laugh, I thought. *I know he loves trees as much as I do. I know he's—*

"As far as you know he could be on the lam from the law. Or a scam artist. A pedophile."

I'd have laughed if the suggestions weren't so malicious. "Don't be ridiculous." I fit nesting teaspoons into each other, checked knives for water spots. "He's a friend to me and a friend to Ebie. Be glad. Be glad for both of us."

"You . . . you tell him things you don't tell me," Russ said. I turned and looked at my husband's back, vulnerable somehow, with his arms raised to the cabinet pulls. "He knew about the smiley face."

My fingers shook a little. One Sunday night I'd

opened the dryer door to fold the last of four loads of laundry, and instead of finding a wrinkled clump of clothing, I'd discovered the dryer empty but for a sheet of paper with a smiley face drawn on it; Russ had finished the laundry for me. I'd told Elliot of Russ's sweet surprise, then immediately worried that Elliot might mention a marital anecdote during lunch that Russ considered intimate. My worry, I realized even then, indicated that the story *was* personal, and that I knew Russ wouldn't like my sharing it.

"I just . . ." Russ said, coming to stand beside me, "*I*'d like to be the one you tell things to. He's a boy. I'm your husband. I'm . . . I was Whit's father."

I plucked a spoon from the scattered silverware on the counter, a battered, deep-dish tablespoon with flowing script on the handle that didn't match the others. "Do you know what this spoon is?"

He looked at it. "I know it was your grand-mother's."

"It's Ebie's favorite spoon. She'd like to eat her cereal with it every day, the way you have a favorite pen, or pillow. Whenever I cleaned out the dish-washer, she'd dive for and claim it. If Whit was home he'd shove her away and grab the spoon and lick it so it was used. Just to drive her crazy. Just because he knew she wanted it." I put the spoon in the drawer. "Did you know that?"

Russ shook his head. "No. Should I?"

I shut the drawer and faced him. "That's the kind of thing I tell Elliot."

"Generic torture," Elliot had smiled, and added, *"Garden-variety sibling atrocity."* "I've told Elliot garden-variety nothings," I told my husband now, using Elliot's apt description.

Russ pulled me against him, and squeezed out the shadow that hovered between us. "Okay," he said. "Okay."

Chapter Nine

I HAD CHRISTMAS MONEY, AND ELLIOT HAD A SECRET Mission, and what Dad had was a fit.

The Secret Mission was Elliot's Christmas present to me, and I didn't even have anything to give him back. Inside a regular Hallmark card he wrote: *I'll drive the car, you pick the destination.* Mom looked at it a long time, like she was one of those people who read fortunes in handwriting, and finally said, "Just like you and Whit." She meant the coupons I used to give him for backrubs and stuff.

We didn't do Christmas cards this year. Mom and Dad had kind of a fight about it. I couldn't decide who was on what side, but I think Dad was *for* using the picture of all of us at Whit's graduation and Mom was *against*. "Can't we just discuss something without the conversation disintegrating?" I heard Dad ask her. Thank goodness for Elliot, who got a part-time job

doing UPS deliveries. In the middle of their discussion
—Dad has told me a thousand times that he and Mom
don't fight, they just *discuss*—Elliot brought a package
to our door so they had to quit *discussing*.

"Do I look like Santa Claus?" Elliot asked, and
both of us laughed because he was wearing a brown
uniform the color of dookey.

"Mom's in a bad mood," Dad said afterward,
which didn't seem fair. Dad was in a bad mood, too,
but he just said it about Mom first, to, like, get me on
his side. I almost wished I could go home with Elliot
for Christmas. I'd really like to see what a pawn shop
looks like.

I didn't mind about the Christmas card, but the
stocking was hard. Mom wanted to put up both
stockings, mine and Whit's. Dad didn't. It's like Mom
wants Whit alive at home, but dead in public, and
Dad wants him alive outside, with other people, but
have him dead at home. I don't know, I've never
been a very good explainer. Like I can't explain why
I thought what Bett said just before Christmas
seemed mean.

"You'll probably get lots more presents this year
since Santa Claus only has to bring stuff to one
person."

I was glad Mom didn't hear that. I'd seen her take
down the big box that sits at the top of her closet all
year where she hides presents. It's a Big Wheel box,

that's how old it is. Her face was red when she took it to the recycling bin, and I knew she'd cried, thinking about the presents she kept in it until this year. Ties and packs of batteries and candy and books and CDs and gift certificates and a belt. Stuff for me, too. She's getting rid of things that remind her too much of Whit. Sometimes it's hard to tell the difference in a bad mood and a sad mood.

"Do you get more presents because there's only one of you?" I said back to Bett.

"But there's *always* been only one at my house," she said.

She got a pony-skin Indiana Jones hat that she told me cost a hundred and ten dollars, and a real pager. But here's what I got and it is *awesome*: my own video cam. Bett and I've been taping ourselves singing, doing advertisements, stuff like that. Bett wants to use it to tape this band she's formed. The band doesn't even have a name and she didn't ask me to be in it, and I don't get it 'cause here I am: a piano player.

Elliot jumped over Meany Matheny's fence one afternoon while Bett and me were taping. He held the cam out in front of his face and talked some gobbledygook language into it, very seriously. "What was that?" I asked.

"The news in Chinese."

"What did you say?"

"Ebie eats her underwear."

Bett and me laughed. Elliot dug keys out of his pocket. "Ready to cash in your Christmas money and my gift certificate?"

You bet I was.

"Do you need to ask your mother?"

I shook my head. If it was Elliot, that would be fine. She loves Elliot.

"Can I come, too?" Bett asked.

"I thought you had band practice," I said. Elliot looked up at the sky and whistled, like characters in cartoons who pretend not to know anything. I slammed the door to Elliot's cop car and the automatic seat belt zipped across my throat and choked me. "Help!"

Elliot laughed and loosened it and wrinkled his nose. "Someone smells like . . ."

I smiled to myself because I knew how good I smelled.

". . . watermelon deodorant and Pine-Sol. Who can it be?"

"Elliot!" I was *affronted*. That's what Anne says all the time. It's from Beatrix Potter. I told him that my New Year's resolution is to use all the body stuff my friends gave me for Christmas. "I have Orange Blossom salt scrub, Ripe Raspberry shower gel, Superlicious Citrus body cream, Vanilla Bean Splash and Cotton Blossom sheet spray. And Berry Fine Bath Oil Beads."

"Your New Year's resolution is suffocating me." He rolled down the car window and hung his head out sideways and gagged and coughed.

"Watch out," I said, but it was too late. The tires banged and the car jumped. We hit smack in the middle of the pothole at the bottom of Liberty Ave. "Mom always swerves around that pothole. It's a habit. Whit always told her not to, that dodging it was dangerous."

"So how was the first week back at school?" Elliot asked.

Well. "Everybody had a lot of new outfits." I was glad Christmas was over. But even if my stocking was gone, I still looked at the nail sticking out from the mantle and remembered how Whit hung his yo-yo there to unwind. "And Bett was Courtney Love for Famous Person Day."

"How do you dress up as Courtney Love?"

"With a grass skirt made out of raffia, like Mom tied some Christmas presents with, and a coconut-shell bra. She told everyone she was the best Famous Person in the whole class."

"Without a flinch of self-irony," Elliot said.

"Huh?" Whenever I start thinking Elliot's my age, he turns into a grown-up again.

"Who did you do?"

I hated telling him. "You've never heard of her. Mom's suggestion."

"Try me."

"Louisa May Alcott."

"I have so heard of her."

"Mom has all her books so I carried them, but I didn't have any good props. I should have been Eloise, but she's a *character* from a book."

"That's famous."

"Not as famous as Jimi Hendrix. That's who came after me. Our next big project is Contemporary Issues."

"And that is?"

"You know, something like gun control, or teenage pregnancy, or drugs or AIDS. Something everybody worries about. I don't know what topic to do mine on."

"Hm," Elliot said. "I know."

"What?"

"It'll be part of our secret mission," he said, and winked. "Decided how to spend your cash yet? A new *ouuutfiiiit*," he said in a drawn-out squeaky make-fun-of voice, "from the *mmaaaaaalll*?"

I've been dying for a million years to get my ears pierced. I've been dying to sit in that purple-and-green plastic ear-piercing throne at Limited Too right next to the window so everyone can see, and put my elbows on the pink desk with the curvy edge and look in the big mirror and let the clerk draw dots on my lobes with a marker and aim that hole-punching pistol at them and do it. "I've asked Mom forever if I could pierce my ears, but—"

"But what?"

"She's always said no." *No no no not until you're thirteen*, which is like waiting for hair to grow. "But today when I asked for the thousandth time Mom didn't even stop sweeping the kitchen. She said, 'Go ahead.' Not 'yes' just . . . 'go ahead.' All of a sudden it seemed like half the reason I begged her was because I knew she'd say no. But now that I can, I don't want to so much anymore."

Elliot put on his polarized sunglasses. "Hate to tell you how many things work out exactly like that, Ebie."

"Like what?"

"Like one of these days you'll have a crush on some boy, and when you find out he likes you back, you won't think he's so great after all."

A crush on a boy? Here's what Whit would say: *Can't see that happening.* My Junior Assembly Valentine dance for middle school grades is coming up. We're allowed to bring guests and I told Dad I was going to bring Bett since she's not a member of the dancing class. "Don't you want to invite a boy?" he'd said.

While I was waiting for our smoothie last week, the counter guy pointed across the store at Bett stacking straws and winked at me. "That your boyfriend?" he asked. Bett's cut her hair even shorter, just like that, didn't even ask her mother. "What I really want," I told Elliot, "is to just be . . . *different.*"

Elliot reached over the steering wheel and shuffled about a thousand pieces of paper slipping around on the dashboard. He pulled one out, slid it across the seat toward me. "Different like this?" he asked and smiled.

But my smile was bigger, so big my chapped lips cracked. "Yes," I said. "Exactly like that."

I looked in the mirror. I looked like an elf, and a rock star, and an island girl and a model and absolutely *nothing* like my old sixth-grade self. Even though the pulling had hurt, I absolutely adored what I looked like, the new me. It had taken almost three hours, but Elliot and me had planned my whole Contemporary Issues project while Glynna did my hair at Leon's Beauty School. EARN WHILE YOU LEARN! the telephone pole advertisement read.

"Do your report on hemorrhagic viruses," he said, "like Ebola. I bet nobody else will do something good as that." I betted not, too.

"Thirty-eight braids times two dollars apiece equals seventy-six dollars," Glynna said.

"But they're skinnies and shorties," Elliot said, "and she didn't get beads, just rubber bands."

Glynna looked at me, thinking. "Well, I've been

doing rows all my life. No talent in that. Okay, I'll only charge you half." I counted out Christmas money from my grandmothers. "I'm training for s*alons*," Glynna said, and slammed the cash drawer shut. "Come back when you want a perm, I'll give you a good deal."

I couldn't stop touching them. In Elliot's car I leaned my head from one shoulder to the other to feel the hard little plaits lying on my cheek like they weren't even my own hair, like they were fake. I looked at myself in Eliot's rearview mirror, put my cheek against the door and looked in the outside mirror, all over. They *were* short, about three inches long, and I loved them. Loved the little white lines of parts on my scalp, loved the silky little tails like paintbrushes, loved the ones that hung over my forehead like clunky bangs. Loved holding a hunk of them in my fist peeking through my fingers like dog's fur. I shook my head to feel them slap my face like fingers playing scales, and remembered just that. "We need to hurry," I told Elliot. "My piano lesson."

I looked up as we turned onto Liberty Ave. A pair of tennis shoes hung over a telephone wire. They'd been dangling up there as long as I could remember, their laces tied together and the two shoes just hanging down. I thought the laces might catch fire—shouldn't they, on a telephone wire? And I thought the person that threw them up there did a

pretty good job to get them there like that, one hanging on either side. "What do those shoes mean?"

Elliot didn't even look. He knew they were
there. He drove under them a hundred times a day
just like we did. "Just that someone wanted to say, 'I
was here.'"

Oh.

Mom bit her lip when she saw my thirty-eight corn
rows. "Where did you get those?"

"At the gettin' place," Elliot said. He held up the
flyer he'd fished out of the dashboard pile, an advertisement for Leon's Beauty School. "See?" he said.
"Some people really do believe the notices on telephone poles."

Mom laughed. I didn't know what they were
talking about—Elliot had gone grown-up again—
but Mrs. Nash drove up anyway, and I had to hurry
inside for my lesson. Halfway through it I looked up.
Elliot was standing just outside the window in our
backyard. He started scratching under his arms like a
monkey then shook a stick at me and opened and
closed his mouth like he was yelling at me for not
practicing, then jumped up and down and pulled
down his eye sockets and ruffled his hair straight out
and leaned back like he was Elvis singing into a
microphone. He wasn't three feet away from us but
Mrs. Nash never noticed him making fun of her

right outside the window while I was playing "Somewhere Over the Rainbow." Luckily, I've memorized it because Mom asks for it so often.

I had to chew on my bottom lip to keep from laughing. Even Whit isn't as funny and smart as Elliot. Wasn't, I mean.

Chapter Ten

THEY WERE JOGGING PAST LIKE UNIFORMED SCHOOL-
children when I opened the bedroom shutters: a
small army of fit male bodies—"Buff," Whit would
say—identically clad in gray T-shirts and navy gym
shorts. I loved happening upon that precisely ranked
formation, legs lifting and dropping in silent unison.
The exercising firemen turned the corner, FIRE bla-
zoned across the backs of their shirts, and I knew.
Even in February, darkest winter, we get balmy, bare-
legged, short-sleeve, open-window days. Gift-from-
God days, someone had remarked that June morning
of Whit's graduation.

Whit.

"Ebie told me you gave Elliot Hatcher a towel for
Christmas," Russ had said the night before.

I sorted bills. "Christmas was weeks ago." I hadn't
not told Russ; I just hadn't told him. The way Whit

would report, "Here are my courses this semester," and we wouldn't discover that he was eligible for Honors history until it was too late to change his schedule. "You had the towel monogrammed," Russ went on.

"The linen store was running a special."

"You don't see anything odd in that gift?"

What would have been odd is if I'd told Russ. Normally he had no interest in the Christmas presents I gave to friends—homemade soup, a bath pillow, a puzzle. Telling Russ of the gift to Elliot would have implied something beyond casual conversation about weekend plans or please put grapefruit on the grocery list or be sure and note Ebie's piano recital on your calendar. *All we talk about are calendars*, Anne had joked so long ago. When Whit's death was so fresh, his absence so intense, my despondency so deep. When even the wheezed rumble of Monday's trash truck sounded like a sigh.

"'Odd'?" I echoed.

Russ took the leather log carrier from its hearth hook. "Well, unusual."

"He's single, probably has nothing decent in the house."

"Whit got a monogrammed towel as a graduation present."

"Did you want me to give him that one?" I heard myself resorting to semantics, detouring around the topic.

Russ unlocked the terrace room door, went outside, and returned with a carrier full of logs.

Ebie looked up from the piano keys, the final chords of "Witchcraft." "Goody, a fire. Let's have popcorn, too."

"I think there's some microwave."

"And Cokes?"

"No Cokes at night."

"You can't have popcorn without Cokes. They go together. Elliot says so."

From within the blackened brick walls of the fireplace Russ said, "My entire family is enamored of the boy next door."

Entire? I thought. *Entire* is three. "Boy?" I repeated. "Enamored? Russ, please."

He wedged a paraffin brick beneath the logs, held a match to it, and said nothing. "Because Elliot's *fun*!" Ebie skipped through the room on her way upstairs, plaits bouncing lightly. "Call me when the popcorn's finished. I'm working on my Contemporary Issues project. "

"Whose idea was those braids?" Russ asked.

⌒

I raised the bathroom mini-blinds. Over the ivy-draped palisade fence, through the branches of the leyland cypress we'd planted to conceal the barefaced brick of Meany Matheny's house, the window across the ivy was suddenly blotted with green. Hunter green with white initials: the towel. Elliot poked his head from around it and waved. I smiled back, embarrassed to be caught looking. Meany Matheny had never glanced out her window. Elliot raised the screen, leaned out, and the twenty feet between us vanished.

I opened our bathroom window. "What are you doing home today?"

His eyebrows lifted. "How soon we forget the infirm. Soaking my injured ankle."

It had been Elliot's idea to spy on Ebie's Valentine dance. "She'll kill us," I'd said.

"She won't know," he replied. We'd crept up to a clubhouse window a foot above our heads. "Curses, foiled again," Elliot had said and, looking around, dragged over a stray cinderblock as a booster step. We'd stood shoulder to shoulder, giggling at the sheer ridiculousness of our caper, and tried to spot Ebie's telltale spiky braids among the dimly lit mass of moving bodies. Until, her eyes wide with horror, Ebie had glimpsed us and we'd ducked and bolted backward, forgetting the stepstool drop off.

"It's sprained," Elliot complained.

"Scraped maybe, but not sprained," I laughed. "Slacker."

When Russ got home from the gym that evening I told him what had happened. Because it was amusing, because I wanted to share it with him. Too, because Ebie was sure to tell him. He'd smiled, adding, "Aren't you a little old for that kind of stunt?"

"Last December when Anne attached a hot-dog penis to the reindeer topiary under cover of darkness, you laughed," I said.

I rattled pens and pencils in a desk drawer, looking for the letter opener. A wedding present.

"Did Elliot give you a Christmas present?" Russ asked.

"He gave *us* one."

"What was it?"

"Mistletoe."

Still stooped on the hearth bricks, Russ craned his head to look at me. "Mistletoe?"

"He works in trees, Russ. It's no different from a florist giving away surplus poinsettias. The crew took down a tree full of mistletoe and Elliot put a box of the stuff on the curb with a sign that said 'Free.'"

Russ stood, braced his arms against the mantle and stared at the flames. "Exactly what is it between you and Elliot Hatcher?"

There's an unwritten rule at Windsor School: If you suspect a boy of wrongdoing—lying, cheating, stealing—you never, ever ask him a direct question.

As a prefect, Whit had explained the reasoning behind it. Windsor worked under a one-shot honor system. A single lie meant expulsion, and if a student is asked a direct question—*Did you take that coat from someone else?*—he may panic, and lie, and compound his infraction. Better to say, *I've never seen that coat before. Is it new?* Better that the boy hears the suspicion; better for everyone that he has time to realize his error, and return the coat to its owner.

"I just want to understand," Russ said.

"Nothing. Friendship."

"Friendship, or kinship?"

I bristled. "What do you mean?"

"It isn't some kind of . . . compensatory love?"

"Is the popcorn ready?" Ebie hollered over the banister.

"You can have Kool-Aid instead of Coke," I told her.

"Elliot calls Kool-Aid rocket fuel," she answered.

From his open window across the ivy Elliot asked, "Today's Ebie's Contemporary Issues presentation at school, isn't it?"

"Yes, on hemorrhagic fevers. She said you'd helped her."

He shrugged. "A little."

A phalanx of trucks rumbled down Liberty Ave—dump trucks, graders, wheeled equipment with no name. Whit would have known. At four, he was fascinated with monster trucks. We'd given him a video that featured nothing but footage of hulking earth-movers at work—backhoes and cranes and front-end loaders—and he'd watched it hypnotically for weeks.

"What's with the commotion?"

"Don't know," I said.

"Let's check it out."

"Lock your door," I warned him. "Warm days bring out the gypsies."

"'Gypsies'?" he repeated with amusement, as though I'd said *cowboys and Indians*, and ducked back indoors.

~

"'Compensatory love'?" I'd repeated back to Russ. "Don't be absurd. Elliot's a friend. He's *everybody's* friend. Anne's friend, Ebie's friend, Mack and Diego and Teddy Strickland's friend—"

"Teddy who?" and didn't wait for an answer. "Elliott is half your age."

"Last time I counted, twenty-eight was *not* half of forty."

"I mean . . ." Flustered, Russ waved his hands apologetically. "He's halfway between your age and Whit's age."

I knew Russ was trying to articulate something

difficult. I sensed his discomfort, his reluctance. And I ignored it. "So?"

"Do you see anything . . . symmetrical in this? Graduation-type gifts, his youth, Whit's de—Whit not being here."

When you need to occupy yourself, to avoid a topic that prickles or threatens, there's always household minutiae, invented or postponed trivial tasks to occupy you as he follows you around and talks at you. You water a houseplant, put up dried dishes in the sink, check the detergent supply in the storage closet, put away Ebie's sheet music.

It was an unremarkable house on a corner lot. Though I drove past it each day I didn't know the owners of the cream-colored brick home with a charcoal roof and S-curve front walk between boxwoods so overgrown that my shoulders would have been crowded between them. Diane Monk, a childhood friend, had lived in one of those houses, a fifties split-level whose mid-story landing, four steps between the kitchen and her bedroom, I found clever and enviable when I visited her.

Unsure what we were witnessing, Elliot and I watched as the English box were roped off with flimsy yellow caution tape. A bulldozer snorted and lunged forward, lifting the huge bushes from the earth and depositing them in a pathetic huddle near the curb like houseplants past their prime, put out-side to be dealt with later. We watched as raw lumber support beams were wedged beneath the porch roof. Watched as the wrought-iron grillwork on the front porch was unscrewed, unsoldered, the process as alien to me as watching a tree come down. Until Elliot had explained and humanized it for me.

"They're redoing their entrance," I guessed. Guessed wrong. Others had joined us now, walkers, mothers with small children killing time before naps with this accidental entertainment. Far better than watching the too-ordinary garbage truck, which itself had pulled over to observe. Even the city leaf truck, completing its final curbside pickup of the season a month before spring's official beginning, paused to watch.

The bulldozer reversed and was joined by another that gutturally roared into action, obliter-ating conversation as it belched diesel stink into the warm February air. And then, intent became terribly clear. The house was being leveled, razed, destroyed. Not because it was condemned. Not because the mortgage wasn't paid. Not because it stood in a flood zone. Just *because*.

The destruction would have been fascinating if it weren't so disturbing, witnessing iron-teethed machines plow into walls as if they were no thicker, no stronger, no more solid and resistant than the blocks—triangles, squares, rectangles—Whit had played with as a toddler. Sections of roof caved in on rooms that people had lived and loved and eaten and slept and wept in. The mighty machinery pillaged and plundered, exposing the cream-colored painted bricks as pretenders, ordinary red brick. They left great slabs of broken sidewalk in their gobbling wake, jagged chunks still bearing initials of children, the indelible spirals of fireworks snakes. Dust billowed from sheetrock and concrete and brick, from splintered wood and fall-drought earth.

Two bulldozers, two hours; three dump trucks, three hours. Those are the statistics that reduce a house to a rubble pile. Someone's *home*. With wall dents gouged by doorknobs; with brighter rectangles where pictures hung undisturbed for years; with shelf paper in the cabinets and door frames with height hash marks; with fingerprints above the landing and scuff marks of Christmas tree tops on the ceiling.

Gone. So swiftly gone, like—

We watched the postmortems, Elliot and I. Waited as others left, wandered away, got on with their lives. Watched as the remains were gathered, reduced from bulk to debris, forked into dump trucks and hauled away in a mere two loads. Until all that remained was a flattened square of land, curiously brown earth, healthy and rich-looking, the tracks of machinery across it neat and symmetrical as plowed rows in a field. A humble piece of land, conversely smaller without the poor house upon it than with it, now so clearly, cleanly defined: A Lot.

"Incredible," Elliot said finally, as we turned away from the stunning transformation. "How something is there, and then just . . . not."

Like Whit.

When we reached his house, Elliot said, "*My* house is a lot uglier than the one they took down." True enough. He looked at me, his black wiry curls speckled with mortar dust, the way drifting sawdust had settled there the afternoon I'd gone to the Strickland farm with him. "I know what we need." His smile was shy, sheepish. "Wanna get high?"

⌒

Russ leaned against the refrigerator. "You seem overly . . . *familiar* with Elliot."

"'Familiar'?" I repeated. "Yet it's okay for you to speculate with Darrell about whether someone's had a boob job?" Russ shifted, knocking off an Oreo magnet. I knelt to retrieve it and looked up at him. "Do you *object* to my friendship with Elliot?"

"I think you're susceptible, and vulnerable. You've lost a child, your son. What's happening between you and Elliot is—I worry that you've transferred . . ." he put his hand on mine as I dug a tablespoon into the carton of instant potatoes.

"Watch out, it'll spill," I said and stirred the pale flakes into the bowl of bread starter. *Three tablespoons potato flakes, one half cup warm water.* Any number of things needed doing, and I pulled out the coupon file to look for date-expired ones. **Cleaners, Paper Products, Breakfast Foods, Sweets,** read the tabbed dividers.

"He's so much like Whit," Russ went on.

I snapped the elastic around the file, moved to the pantry. The napkin stack needed refilling. We were low on sugar and—

"Has this crossed your mind, Laura? Elliot is young like Whit, he's lively like Whit, he's—look at his hair."

"Hair?" I shoved the drawer shut and swiveled to face Russ. "What are you going to say next, Russ? That both their names end with t?"

⁓

Even after twenty years it comes back to you. Even if you'd been a drinker, not a toker, who preferred the liquid-courage, good-tasting effects of alcohol to the dreamy, floating, quasi-trance effects of marijuana. Pinching the joint, holding your breath, shutting your eyes to the lazy stinging smoke, the sweetish unmistakable smell. The loosening. It all comes back.

Languorously high, I surveyed surroundings I'd never seen but was nevertheless familiar with. The room was a near duplicate of a Windsor School dorm commons. The cheap tweedy sofa with minimally upholstered arms stood between two collapsible nylon chairs identical to the one in Whit's closet, still neatly packed in its cylindrical carrier with a gift bow attached to the handle. Opposite the sofa was a recliner whose seat was patched with parallel rows of silver duct tape.

"Faux Naugahyde," Elliot said cheerfully, "Army town pawn shop furniture."

The coffee table, though, was a unique, gorgeous thing: a flat, thick, smoothly patina'd cross-section of tree trunk more than two feet wide. A tree, of course, and bare of anything but its natural beauty. I ran my finger over the surface, feeling no grain beneath the glossy lacquer, then fit my fingers into the rough bark at the edges. "This is so gorgeous."

"Black walnut. Woodworkers covet black walnut. This table is the only thing I own worth anything. The tree was over a hundred years old, and grew in our yard."

A hundred years. "Tell me."

"It had to come down. That was painful."

"Why?"

"Its value. Mother needed money since my father was . . . wasn't around."

I wordlessly took the proffered joint.

"But black walnut trees . . ." Elliot paused, and I wondered if dope or memories was behind his hesitation. "Their roots secrete a toxic substance, so that a black walnut eventually kills anything growing in a twenty-foot radius. Highly prized but highly poisonous. Can't have the good without the bad." He shrugged away his introspection and leaned forward to swipe nonexistent dust from the beautiful wooden slab. "I don't have much sitting-around stuff."

I leaned my head against the sofa back, feeling the scratchy material prickling my neck, and watched the smoke pool at the ceiling. I'd forgotten that, the heightened awareness.

Elliot followed my gaze. "But I do have a fried bug collection inside the bosom ceiling lamp. Or half-bosom, complete with nipple." I laughed at his accurate description of the hideous fixture, a milky glass hemisphere with a dubiously decorative brass knob in its dead center. The faint uneven silhouette of insect bodies within the glazed glass was soft and mothy, literally and figuratively.

~

"I don't know what the term is." Russ had gone on trying. I'd gone on, too, washed soap scum from the hand pump, refolded the blanket throw on the sofa.

"Transference or replacement or displacement behavior or projection. Some unhealthy sort of self-therapy—"

"Which psychospeak is it, Russ? Maybe there's a neurosis or two that you've overlooked. One that might apply to you. Paranoia, for instance. Have you ever considered just calling it *friendship*?"

He followed me to the dryer, chuckled casually. "It's occurred to me that we might adopt—"

Fingers on the lint trap, I pivoted, aghast. "You'd try to replace Whit?"

Russ held up his palms, victorious finally in stopping my pointless chores and claiming my full attention, but acknowledging that he was only *teasing*. "Not at all. Why should we? We've already adopted Elliot Hatcher."

⌒

"Want something to drink?" Elliot asked, and I followed him into the small kitchen. My hand paused on the doorknob slung in accumulated rubber bands, and I took in the old round-shouldered refrigerator, the speckled gold linoleum, the metal-banded countertops and spindly dinette set. He opened a cabinet, revealing a dozen plastic cups bearing NASCAR race dates, movie tie-ins, sports team logos: give-aways and freebies from fast-food stands and discount store refreshment kiosks.

"This is what passes for glassware at my abode," Elliot said apologetically.

It was the dope, of course it was, but the sight of the cluttered, mismatched collection touched me. Once, as a young wife, I'd searched for a glass in Anne's kitchen cabinets and had discovered a similar disarray of shapes and sizes and colors. I'd pictured the matching and unbroken sets of wedding present glasses on my shelves at home and thought, *I'll never let that happen at my house. Not me, no. I'll throw away those kinds of cups.* And then Whit had grown, and wedding present glasses were broken, and he'd brought favors home from birthday parties, and cups from the circus, and Ebie was born, and my youthful arrogance and innocent superiority evaporated and was replaced with my own collection of garish plastic orphan cups that our family used constantly. I rotated a McDonald's cup between my palms and pictured the new glassware in an upstairs room next door: Whit's six graduation mugs.

I sipped Gatorade and looked at our gray siding, our bedroom window, the gulf of ivy. Even in the dead of winter it crept inexorably up the fence posts and tree trunks and heating unit beside the chimney. Even into the lawn, the supposedly civilized yard, stealthily sprouting amid my carefully rooted, carefully tended pachysandra ground covering. In my serene, stoned focus, each ivy leaf seemed sharply visible and each one seemed an affront.

"She likes the low maintenance of ivy," Russ had once said of Meany Matheny. "We can't do anything about it until she's gone."

I blinked away the dope daze and a speck of grit in my eye from the ruined, razed house. Poor house. Poor unsuspecting, vulnerable, done-to house. "I hate that ivy."

Elliot came to stand beside me at the window. "Well, then," he said, "let's *do* it."

⁓

"Finished!" Ebie crowed from the landing. She waved notebook paper covered in her handwriting. "I present my Contemporary Issues report tomorrow and it's going to be the *best*."

I looked up from a basket of catalogs, and Russ looked away from me. "Want to practice the oral part for us?"

She shook her head firmly, turned for her room.

"I don't think you're aware you're doing it," Russ said. "What do you think?"

I didn't ask *Doing what?* "What I think is that he may be an . . . angel. Without him I'd still be, I'd . . ."

"Maybe he's a devil."

"Why don't you look for the good in people?"

"The way you looked for the good in people when they tried to be sympathetic after Whit died?" he countered.

Out went the L.L.Bean, the Lands' End, the J. Crew.

Russ's fingers closed round my upper arm. "Laura!" He'd exhausted the opposing tactics of joking and seriousness, the specific similarities, the analytical suggestions. "Can't you see?" he said in frustration and desperation and accusation. "You're replacing Whit with that boy. You're making Elliot Hatcher your son!"

When you're purging, the beginning is easy. Scuffed sandals, shoes that pinch, toe-hole tennies: simple. The too-short skirt, the stained sweater, the underwear with exhausted elastic. From the desk go school rosters from the previous year, mechanical pencils lacking lead, capless markers. Purging ivy is just the same.

The loose top layer ripped away in long ropy strands. It had no grip, no ground, no foothold; lay like a jump rope for the taking. We didn't even pause to stand, just laughed as we spread our legs wide to cover the most territory, and greedily grabbed anything within reach from our stooped position, stripping and pulling. We laughed with the second layer, too, picking up a strand as in a child's party game of following a trail. We yanked it from the ground, pursuing it when it broke as if trailing a criminal to the border. The heap of leafy vines behind us grew higher as one of us waded from the thinning green patch between our houses to add another fistful.

It's the later purging that's harder. Easy decisions yield to difficult choices. The expensive blouse that still fits but matches nothing. The belt that's too wide for belt loops but too well made, of good leather, to discard. Jeans too faded to wear but too comfortable to abandon.

So the veiny bottom layer held on, stubborn and tenacious and intractable. Laughter yielded to determination and a kind of personal fury at the hairy stems sucking at tree trunks. My fingernails peeled off as I dug into the rows of stiff clinging ivy cilia, scattering bark chips torn away with the strands. And what I couldn't rip away, I chopped off at the base where the vine had unwisely left mother earth to climb the tree. I wanted that ivy to die, wanted to sever the parasite from life support and watch it shrivel on the trunk. With the aroma of damp dirt rising from the torn ground, reefer reek rose from me, or from Elliot, flailing with an intensity equal to mine. We must have looked like banshees, intent and grim, savagely clawing the earth seeking the last blind rootlet of ivy, hunting down its offspring and grandchildren and great-grandchildren still pale and hidden in the earth, supposedly safe.

The ground—so shallow now, without the

decades-old foot-deep blanket of ivy—seemed not pathetic and naked, like The Lot on the corner, but freed, I thought, liberated at last from ivied bondage. Despite calves grimed with dirt, bloodied nails, ruined tennis shoes, and my T-shirt dark with sweat and grime, I stood triumphant and purified in the choppy, moist dark earth. I looked at Elliot as he, too, straightened, stretched, and we laughed, fell backward into that pile of harmless vines, thick and springy as a mattress.

"Better than a leaf pile," he said.

"Much." I raised my hands, considered a bleeding cuticle.

"Nice manicure," Elliot observed.

Are these old lady shoes? I'd asked Whit. *They would be if you were an old lady.*

I staggered up, trailing vines like Ophelia. *Haven't you noticed?* Russ had asked me. *He's so like Whit.* "I need a Band-Aid."

But the front and kitchen and terrace doors were locked against gypsies, just as I'd intended, and locking me out. Elliot was unconcerned. "So we break in. Come on."

I stood beneath the kitchen window seven feet above my head, the only downstairs window not fitted with bolt devices on the sashes, so I could open it while I washed or stirred, or let cooking smells out. Elliot dragged a chair from the terrace to stand on and I struggled to loosen the screen, which clattered down to the driveway when I finally forced it out. I raised the glass, looked down at Elliot. "Help."

"Give me some room," he said, and climbed onto the chair seat meant for one rump, not two bodies and four feet. I jumped, and he caught my legs and hoisted me to the sill, where I immediately knocked a small vase, a bottle of vitamins, and two pale winter tomatoes into the sink.

Which is how Russ, dropping by, found the two of us: sweaty, filthy, bedraggled, partially stoned, and laughing, my butt wagging from a window of my own house we'd broken into, with Elliot holding my dirty dangling legs, wearing a laurel of ivy on his black curls like a conquering hero. A scene from somewhere between the Keystone Kops and a French farce.

Which is how Ebie, getting off the bus, found us, too. I hardly recognized my child. Her hair was unplaited, ruffling almost perpendicularly out from her head in a Cleopatra pyramid. But it was her mouth and chin the three of us stared at. Dried blood ran from reddened lips to her chin and down her neck in irregular streaks.

"Ebie!" I cried, fear sobering me instantly. It looked as though she'd been assaulted. "Are you okay?" Though clearly she was, despite the bloody drops on her shirt and smears on her collar. "What happened?"

Russ looked from me to Ebie, to me again, to her, as though he recognized neither of us. And then he looked across the yard at the waist-high mound of tangled vines, and the denuded ground scattered with torn ivy leaves and chunks of upturned earth. "Will someone please tell me what is going on?"

Ebie, though, grinned around fuchsia teeth and gums. "It's from the pills Elliot got for my report on hemorrhagic viruses." Then the grin faded. "But Mrs. Evans got mad. She sent home a note."

"Pills?" Russ asked, confused.

"Blood capsules like they use in the movies. I hid them in my cheek and bit down on them during my oral report and fake blood squirted out everywhere, just like it happens when people have Ebola. Mrs. Evans about fainted. That's why I got a note."

I bit my knuckle to keep from laughing.

"Yes," Elliot said with utter seriousness, "but did you get an A?"

Chapter Eleven

"WHAT HAPPENED, DID YOU GET FIRED?" I CALLED TO RUSS.
It was an old joke, a question I asked whenever he
managed to arrive home early enough to join me and
the children for dinner. When it was *children,* not *child.*

Halfway out of his car, Russ stopped. He leaned
in again, retrieved a batch of papers from the front
seat, and walked up the driveway. "I was in the neighborhood and just decided to come home early."

"You were? Doing what?"

"I—overseeing a crew."

I leaned into my own car, brushed pine needles
from the back seat. "Since when do you have a crew
in Winwood?"

"What's with the pine needles?"

Proud of my afternoon's efforts, I pointed across
the yard at a thick russet quilt. It had taken eight bales
of pine straw to cover the ivy-shorn twenty-foot strip

between our yard and Elliot's. "Almost as good a job as the professional fluffers, don't you think?" I asked Russ. Through the years I'd been by turn envious, irritated, and amused by landscaping teams hired by homeowners specifically to freshen and replenish pine needles in borders. "Anne says it looks like the houses are sitting in rusty snow drifts." I pulled Ebie's backpack from the car, where she'd left it in her hurry to answer the phone. "Not likely, with the kind of weather we're having. The robins are even back," I told Russ, feeling warm and expansive with accomplishment. Though Elliot had laughingly informed me otherwise.

"The robins aren't *back*," he'd said from the split rail fence where he sat lazily watching me labor. "They're ground feeders. They go wherever the ground is thawed enough to get at a worm."

"How'd you know that?" I'd asked him.

"I work with birds," he'd said, "in trees. Remember?"

"And warm enough for people to be out of their houses," I said to Russ. "Someone rang Leigh Brabson's doorbell twice yesterday, but she was in the basement and couldn't answer it. When she came upstairs there were two strangers standing in her living room who claimed they were conducting a survey. Sure they were. They were conducting a survey of who was at home before they cleaned it out. But what could Leigh accuse them of?"

Russ leaned against the car. "Sometimes we get our worst snows in March."

"What? Oh, that reminds me. We need to discuss which week this summer will be best for Anne and Darrell and put down a deposit on the beach house rental before it gets booked." I was proud all over again because there'd been a time when I thought I could never return to the place Whit and I had been heading, never even want to drive that stretch of road again. I hadn't, yet, but I would. I was getting there.

"Where's Ebie?" Russ asked.

"Bett doesn't have band practice this afternoon so she's graced Ebie with her presence."

Though I'd tried to tell Ebie to seek out other friends and not wait for Bett's attention, Ebie had heard the phone ringing from the open window and sprinted indoors, chanting, "I hope it's her, I hope it's her." As if I were counseling Ebie to *play it cool*, and as if Ebie would understand such a ploy. "So about the beach house . . ."

Russ made a doubtful noise. "I don't think—it's probably not a good idea to make any summer plans with the McCalls."

"Why not? I thought you'd be glad that I was, that I could . . . move on. Cleaning the tool shed is next on my list."

"You haven't cleaned out Whit's room."

Something that had softened inside me began to harden again. "Cleaned?"

He gazed at the yard, said finally, "You really think it looks better without the ivy?"

"I think it *will* look better, eventually, now that the pachysandra has room to grow." When he didn't answer I said, "Everything else is being ripped up or torn down, like that poor house on the corner. Why not the ivy?"

Russ furled a set of blueprints. "That corner house was architecturally nondescript. Not a cottage, not even a ranch."

"I heard the reason those beautiful trees were cut down is because the new owners want to install a, quote, 'authentic English garden.'" Though *heard from Elliot* was more precisely correct. "Why 'grow' flowers when you can 'install' them? Cart off the trees, bring on the Canterbury bells." I shook my head.

"The trees had to go because gardens need sun."

"English gardens don't grow in North Carolina. We're hot, we're dry, we're clay. Whose side are you on?"

"I didn't know there were sides."

Puzzled, I shut the trunk.

"Why did you park this way?" Russ asked. "You took up the entire driveway."

Because I'd needed the car's height to stand on

and replace the screen still leaning against the trash can. The screen I'd intended to replace in the window before Russ came home and was reminded of the sight of me hanging from the kitchen window that marijuana-dazed afternoon.

And yet . . . our first introduction had been under the influence. I looked at Russ's familiar profile—the straight nose and wide brow and squared chin, a handsome man—and remembered a September afternoon in a fraternity house bedroom whose cinderblock walls were draped with wrinkled batik bedspreads. A doorless closet exposed a sagging dowel crammed with shirts on wire hangers above a jumbled mess of shoes, huge and male and brown. The warmest appointment in the room was a terrarium in which an inert snake slumbered beneath a heat lamp.

I was a brand-new freshman who knew one of the "brothers" from my home town. Russ Lucas was a worldly sophomore I'd never met. The snake's owner had produced two joints, and five of us—Russ, me, and three others—had sat on the filthy rug and smoked them. I'd wanted so badly to be part of it, wanted equally badly not to appear the green girl that I was. We sat and smoked wordlessly, I wondering what I was meant to feel even as I focused intently on the silky pink tassels of my peasant blouse. They seemed to dangle prettily against my bare, tanned upper arms. Then Russ had pointed to my breasts and asked cheerfully, "Are you wearing a bra?"

I wasn't. Even making the decision to go braless had felt fabulously liberated, sexy, and collegiate. The peasant blouse was thin but not sheer; I'd be mysteriously tempting. And here was Russ with his straight-out question born of weed and curiosity.

I'd fallen in love with that blithe, genial candor.

"So I could put the screen back in the window," I told the man I married. Holding it, I climbed on the car hood and changed the subject. "Remember the day I found Whit jumping up and down on the roof of our old Toyota, pretending it was a trampoline? Except that there wasn't any bounce, just dents. Remember? The roof was so caved in we couldn't sit inside the car! Whit was about six, plenty heavy."

"I remember insurance wouldn't pay for it." His tone was clipped.

I snapped in the screen and peered at him. "What's wrong, Russ?"

"Hard day." He cleared his throat. "Sad day, rather."

"Why?"

"Because of Darrell."

"Is something wrong with Darrell?"

Russ shuffled the papers in his arms. "He's leaving Lucas Con."

"What?" I slowly sat down on the car hood.

"Why? You've been partners for—" I had to stop and count— "fifteen years."

"Not equal partners. You know that. I'm the owner."

"Isn't Lucas making money? Is that it? There isn't enough to support us all? But that's impossible, busy as you are."

It wasn't Russ's habit, had never been part of our conversations, to discuss specific projects with me. A contractor has a dozen construction deals simultaneously in play, with all their attendant problems—owner complaints, plumbing and HVAC and roofer no-shows, weather delays, delivery and inspection postponements, code and zoning hearings. Russ and Darrell spent their days in new subdivisions springing up beyond city limits, transforming countryside into suburbs on streets too new to be included on city maps.

"No, not that." Russ shook his head. "This has been coming for a while. Darrell and I want the company to go in different directions. We've developed different interests."

"What directions? What do you mean?"

Russ visibly hesitated, his expression complex and unreadable. "And Darrell's ... done some things." He walked up the kitchen steps as I stood dumbfounded in the driveway, the implications spinning themselves into reality. Our best couple friends. Russ's closest friend.

"Such as what?"

Russ lifted a shoulder, winced. "Given bonuses to some employees over others. Favored certain contractors."

"But haven't you done that, too? Isn't that part of the business?" I struggled to comprehend. Darrell McCall had always been there with his kind, unassuming mien, his reticent nature, the soft-spoken side of Lucas Con. "The undertaker," I sometimes fondly referred to him, "Mr. Serious." Teasing but affectionate nicknames for Anne's alter ego. Darrell, whose quiet presence I loved. Darrell, whom I'd hardly seen since Whit died and since I withdrew.

I slid off the car. "He didn't screw up some major contract, or embezzle payroll, or come to work drunk. You don't part ways over the things you mentioned. You don't rip up a relationship that's both personal and professional because of—"

"It's a cumulative effect, Laura. And it wasn't a unilateral decision. Darrell agreed to it." Russ opened the kitchen door and went inside. "I'm thinking bigger-picture, more long-term, and Darrell would be content with kitchen remodels and bathroom additions for the rest of his days. He's simply no longer the right man for the job."

I followed him to the sink. "So Darrell is leaving because he's found a job he prefers more?" It wasn't adding up.

"No, but he will. He'll find a position with a builder he's better suited to, on the same page with. Contractors are busier than ever, you said so yourself."

"What about his income until then?"

Russ washed his hands. "Darrell isn't poor. He's principled. Or so he thinks."

"What do you mean?"

"Well, that business with his car, for example."

To the horror of his wife and daughter, Darrell drove a woody wagon with over two hundred thousand miles on the odometer. Adele and Anne refused to ride in it. "It's like a man spending his last dollar on a wallet," Anne remarked when her husband had the seats releathered at a specialty automotive shop. Darrell was as oblivious to the vintage MGs and two-seater Triumphs in the upholsterer's bays as he was to his women's mortification.

"The spin is that the decision is mutual."

"Spin?"

"There'll have to be some kind of announcement. To keep office morale high we haven't told anyone yet."

"But it's not that Darrell isn't producing, it's that—" Panic rose with a slow dawning. "Wait a minute. So it *isn't* mutual. Did you . . . You *fired* your best friend. Is that what you've done?"

"*No*. Darrell and I are . . . separating. This isn't

personal, it's business." Russ calmly dried his hands on a dishtowel. I spoke to his shoulders.

"But Russ, Anne and Darrell—we live on the same street, in the same neighborhood! We've raised our children together. Whit and Adele, Anne and I, we have a history together. So many years and—" From a constricted throat my voice was small. "Christmases and Thanksgivings and beach weeks . . . all the ordinary days of simply living, seeing one another and—"

He interrupted. "Since when? It's not like you've been out there since—" he lowered his voice, "since Whit died."

"But I am now, I am now!"

"Thanks to who?" Russ reached into the slanting windowsill, open to the springlike air, and picked up a beige wooden ball, dirty and pocked.

I took a deep breath and spoke slowly. "I cannot believe that you're doing this to your closest friend, to *our* closest friends. The Russ Lucas I know wouldn't be capable of this."

Russ swiveled to face me, his movement as deliberate and paced as my voice. "And maybe you don't know Darrell McCall either."

"What's that supposed to mean?"

His knuckles whitened over the ball. "There's an ugly aspect to the whole matter. It has to do with Sherry."

Sherry Weaver was Lucas Con's receptionist, typist, administrative assistant, all-around and indispensable Gal Friday. Sunny, single, strawberry blonde Sherry answered when Anne or I phoned the office. We joked that Sherry saw more of our spouses, knew more of their whereabouts, closet contents, and bathroom habits, than we did. "Next of kin," Anne and I called Sherry, and addressed the tags of Christmas and Secretary's Day gifts that way as well. We were grateful that she fielded our questions, reminded our husbands of approaching anniversaries, filed our insurance claims, typed or copied children's school reports. "If Sherry's the employee Darrell gave the higher bonus to, she deserves it and more," I said.

"Darrell and Sherry are . . ."

Russ faltered, stopped short of uttering the phrase that alters everything. *Having an affair.* Tawdry, talk-show term, clichéd and common as the situation it described. *Cheating on his wife.* I shut my eyes to the vision of Darrell and Sherry rising ineluctably before me. Oh, Darrell, no.

"They're very . . . close," Russ said. "It's obvious to everyone that they have a relationship that goes beyond office bantering and . . ."

Oh, Darrell. Foolish Darrell. Sweet, affable Darrell with the slight paunch and ready hug, the good citizen who put out his American flag every national holiday. I grabbed at a straw. "You don't *know* they're involved."

Russ's eyes bored into mine. "No, I don't *know*. I only *know* that the entire office and most of the sub-contractors are talking about it, speculating, or grumbling. Want me to ask Darrell outright? Would *you*?" he challenged me.

I looked down, away from the demeaning picture of Russ confronting Darrell like a father with a misbehaving child or a police officer questioning a suspect. Away from this explicit illustration of Windsor's direct question theory, of forcing someone to lie, or deny, or stammer a confession. I felt weak, enervated, my earlier joy in yard work and the surging anger at Russ both vanished. "Verge-a-tears," Anne would say, and normally I'd laugh.

Anne. Caustic, pragmatic, and innocent Anne. We'd walked for the first time in months today, easy with each other again. A gray pickup had passed us, then cruised by again, and we'd assumed it was a building crew of some sort—painters or alarm installers—searching for an address. But the two young men, no more than twenty-five or twenty-six, had braked and beckoned to us, shown us IDs. They were undercover cops patrolling Liberty Ave and neighboring streets for suspicious characters following Leigh Brabson's report.

"Be careful of B-and-Es," the sunglassed driver

had warned, and explained the thieves' procedure. "These people park and watch from binoculars until folks leave their houses and then break in, though unlocked houses make them very happy. You ought to walk with a cell phone in case you see anything suspicious. Here's our phone number."

They'd nodded and pulled away from the curb. "S-and-M I know, but what's B-and-E?" Anne said.

I'd thought a minute. "Breaking and entering!"

We'd giggled. "Those two guys probably looked at the assignment sheet this morning and said, 'Oh boy, landed the high cotton, low IQ beat today.'"

"We must've looked like Lucy and Ethel," Anne said, and we'd laughed at the picture, a couple of housewives turned law-enforcement accomplices. Oh, Anne. "Cheap and cheerful Sherry," Anne occasionally called Sherry. Sherry wasn't delighted by something; instead she was *tickled*.

"But suppose it *is* only a rumor," I said to Russ now. "Suppose it's not true?"

"A rumor can be as damaging as a fact. That's what I mean by poor morale. It's bad for everything. Besides, where there's smoke there's usually some kind of fire."

"Does Anne know?"

Russ's eyebrows lifted with both sympathy and disbelief at my ignorance. "You walked with her today. What do you think? Who'll tell her?"

A fresh set of realizations took shape and accosted me with a classic moral quandary. Who indeed. A trusted friend? That would be me. Difficult as it was to imagine, Darrell's affair was far more imaginable than telling Anne about it. Whatever I did would be wrong. "You're lying," she'd scorch me. "Why didn't you tell me?" she'd blast me later if I didn't.

Russ tossed the ball from hand to hand. I waited for him to recognize the chipped, dented, earth-stained wooden sphere whose double stripes had faded. The ball had been part of Whit's croquet set, part of our summer evenings past, with lemonade and gin and tonics and fireflies and step-sitting with Anne and Darrell. A croquet set missing at least one of its balls had been left long ago to the Sunday night curbside scavengers. The battered ball I'd found buried in the ivy that day of the razed, done-to house had seemed both poignant treasure and cruel reminder. The razed, done-to ivy day when the robins had come back and I'd felt vibrant and vital and . . . happy.

I waited. Suddenly it seemed critical and imperative that Russ recognize the object he was idly palming—that he smile, and name it, and remember those days, too.

"What's this?" he said and casually held up the scarred wooden ball. "What's the point of saving it?"

Chapter Twelve

My nightgown clung to my stomach and thighs like draped garments on a Greek marble statue, and though I absently pulled at the crackling fabric it drifted back to my skin as if magnetized. Outside the window, pachysandra and liriope leaves stiffened by the frigid nighttime temperatures seemed to stretch for the morning sun making its slanted path around the house's corner. Behind me the television weatherman bemoaned a summer drought that had endured through autumn and into winter, leaving the March air so cold and dry that we shrank from touching car handles and doorknobs and one another. When I clicked it off, the television rewarded me with an electric shock.

Not even the weathermen could decide afterward whether it was freezing rain or sleet.

"Sleet and freezing rain are the same thing," I said.

"Not to tree people," Elliot said.

"They are to a layman."

"Lay *person*."

"It's the same to me," Ebie simply informed the two of us, "because school shuts down for both."

The sound of falling ice is a dry, impersonal noise. Sleet sounds like what it is, *slit tit slit tit*, a faint papery rattle. Like slivers of freezing rain, its accumulation is lethal on streets and steps, but so very very beautiful, transforming a bleak winter landscape into a crystalline otherworld scene from Tolkien. Icy shellac glazed clusters of red pyracantha berries so thickly that they drooped with their burden, too crusted even for birds' sharp beaks. Evergreens became statuesque gentlewomen clothed in ice crinolines. The thinnest tree branch was so slickly sheathed that in the sun's irradiating glare that single day between storms, the bare branch was invisible inside its glittering prison of ice.

And then, a day later, snow. Forecasters had recovered their self-esteem and confidence, drawn themselves up and predicted—not to worry—an inch. But the storm stalled over South Carolina, and a high-pressure system lingered along the coast, and the jet stream pushed cold temperatures northward, and the new moisture in the atmosphere couldn't go anywhere but down. Thus the classic setup for a foot-deep, thirty-six-hour dumping.

"Joy in Mudville!" Elliot crowed.

We're permitted to love snow here, allowed to be childishly thrilled. Substantial snowfalls are so infrequent that no one's prepared, and because everything comes to a halt we've learned it's best to enjoy snow, not fight it. You can tell natives from transplants when it snows: the grown-ups playing outside are Southerners. Or perhaps they're just children at heart.

I spun the pantry lazy Susan, hoping the hot chocolate mix hadn't hardened into concrete. No one would be going to a grocery store or anywhere else without chains or a four-wheel-drive. I love being marooned, and the cozy housebound chaos snow bestows: the jumble of jackets and scarves and boots dug from closets and drawers, a daylong fire, damp clothing tumbling in the dryer, snowmelt puddles on the kitchen floor, rooms redolent of wood smoke and drying wool.

There was the chocolate mix, still powdery, beside of bag of mini-marshmallows dried to pellets. "Northwood is the best street for sledding."

"I know," Ebie said and pulled on gloves.

"Maybe I'll come with you."

She paused meaningfully, conveying the full extent of her horror. "Mom. I would die."

No, I thought, *you will not die. You will not die in an accident and you will not die of mortification. You are all I have left.* "Wear a hat," I said, and pulled one over her head. "More heat is lost through your noggin than anywhere else."

"It itches my forehead," Ebie said. She yanked off the scratchy wool toboggan and electrified hair rose round her face like a nimbus. She licked her palms, flattened the flyaways to satisfaction, and left me. From the window I watched her legs, fattened by purple down bib overalls, grow smaller as she trudged toward Bett's house.

When your children are young you take them sledding, and the reasons for being out in the snow are legitimate. But there's no good justification for playing alone in the snow once your children are grown. Or gone.

No, I wouldn't go there.

I roamed the house, appreciating rooms made lighter by the white world beyond the panes. But I was restless, longed to *do* something, something out-side. The boxwoods at the front of the house were splayed beneath snow as though a giant outstretched hand had mashed them. I pulled on boots and coat, and knocked away the snow with clumsy swats of a broom. The shrubs' dark green branches sprang upward, freed from the heavy blanket. I admired the single vertical stripe of wind-blown snowfall on tree trunks as if they'd shouldered their way into the storm, the crystal hieroglyphics on the snow of fallen ice from thin branches overhead, and terrace chairs whose every wrought-iron curlicue was decorated with its own white icing. No chef or calligrapher could have performed the job more professionally than Mother Nature. I refilled the birdfeeder for the titmice and juncos in their tidy gray suits and brown vests, then cast about for another task, reluctant to clean the car windshields. Not because it would be a nigh impossible task given the bedrock layer of ice varnish beneath the snow, but because I wasn't interested in battling or besting the weather and its effects. I wanted to be *part* of it, not hasten its disappearance.

But shoveling the front walk wasn't cooperating with the sourpusses who grumbled about snow's inconvenience, was it? I'd be performing a kindness for the dark-of-night appointed rounds.

"Where's Russ?" Elliot called, and stepped over the fence reduced to a single rail by the snow's depth. "Isn't shoveling his job?"

I stretched muscles already tender from unaccustomed exercise. "Mailmen have nothing on Russ. He went to work." A Lucas Con employee, giddy with the opportunity to strut his automotive stuff, had come by in a mammoth SUV to pick up Russ. But the snow had stopped workmen, barred carpenters and bricklayers and plumbers and electricians from their daily assaults on Liberty Ave construction sites. "Whatever happened to the days when boys came around and offered to shovel your walk?"

"What days were those?" Elliot asked all innocence. "I don't think I was alive then."

Probably not, I thought. "The stuff of fiction, Dick and Jane."

"Who?"

"Cut it out. You've heard of them."

"Don't shovel. Shoveling is the same thing as wishing the snow was gone."

I looked across the street into a backyard where a trampoline sagged with an impossibly level layer of white weight. He was so right. Snow's time is so short, its beauty as brief as—as a child's life. You have to love it while you can, while it's there. I knelt and scooped a ball of snow, afraid my expression might betray my thoughts.

"I didn't know *anyone* still wore mittens."

He'd done it again: made me smile when sorrow threatened; made me forget. "They do when their daughter steals or soaks all the gloves."

"And what's that over the mittens?"

"Plastic bags, so they don't get wet. I bet you didn't know *anyone* still made a snowman, either." I rolled the ball forward. The snow was perfect for packing, and so deep that no ugly raw streak of ground was exposed. ·

Elliot let himself fall off the fence like the scarecrow in *The Wizard of Oz,* picked himself up, and began rolling his own ball. "Homemade snowmen never turn out like Frosty or Christmas card snowmen."

"They have no personality," I retorted, observing our misshapen spheres. "Snowmen are delicate creatures." I smoothed the hollows, dug my elbow and knee into stubborn lumps, then lifted the smallest of three balls atop the two others and carefully packed snow at the joining. "You can't manhandle them. Their heads will fall off."

"Thanks for the tutorial," Elliot said. He added a head to his snowman and immediately began another. So did I. Then so did he. Then so did I.

Oblivious to the cold, the wet, running noses, hair in eyes, the occasional creeping car, the muffled repetitive *clinksh* of tire chains like sleigh bells three months overdue, we rolled and packed and lifted and shaped and carved and smoothed. Complimenting, criticizing, creating, carping, laughing. Intent and exhilarated, we tramped and stomped back and forth to the house and tool shed for carrots, for a Frisbee or pie plate hat, for stick or tomato stake arms, for sunglasses, for brooms, for stray gloves, for moth-eaten scarves, for visors, for an umbrella, a fright wig.

"The charcoal-for-eyes theory is a crock," Elliot said. "They don't stick."

"Buttons?" I suggested, and though we burrowed

through my sewing box, nothing was large enough. Finally I aimed a tiny bottle of food coloring somewhere in the vicinity of eyes and squirted. "Snowmen have blue eyes, don't they?"

"Now it looks like he's crying," Elliot said as a bright blue stain spread and diluted.

"Excuse me but that he is a *she*. You can tell by the size of her hips."

And somehow there were six snowmen in my front yard. Walkers slowed to look and point and comment. A camera flashed behind us as we worked.

"I hope that was my good side," Elliot said, rising from a crouch.

"I hope it wasn't my butt," I said.

⁓

Ebie had taken up position at the window where the outside thermometer was attached. "You'll never be able to see it happen," I warned her. After a few afternoon hours of above-freezing temperatures the mercury was predicted to fall into the low twenties and she was convinced she'd be able to watch the crimson line actually shorten. "It's too gradual," I said, "like leaves coming out on the trees."

Russ was worried about ice damming, melted water refreezing and jamming the gutters so that water seeped inside. "Doesn't help matters that our gutters have needed replacing for two years."

"We're like the cobbler's children," I replied, and asked Ebie, "How was the sledding on Northwood?"

She rolled her head back and forth on the pane. "I liked Bett better when she was just *my* friend."

"What do you mean?"

"She's met some other people and now they call her up all the time and they came to Northwood too, and I just . . ." She wiped at the smudge left on the glass.

"Don't like sharing her?"

The frown indicated that she'd heard me, but didn't like the question. "I just want Bett to be . . . mine."

"Play me something on the piano," I suggested. "Play 'What a Wonderful World.'" I leaned to stow away the Dutch oven, one of Elliot's not-so-bright ideas for a hat. It had smushed the head and left a rust-colored rim.

"So this one's a monk," he'd shrugged, "with a fringe of auburn hair."

"It's called a 'tonsure,'" I'd told him. I closed the cabinet on the heavy cast-iron cauldron, and massaged my back.

"Your back hurt?" Russ asked, noticing.

"Must be from shoveling."

"Or building a half dozen snowmen," he said mildly.

I was saved not by a bell but a single loud *crack* somewhere in the neighborhood, a retort audible in the stillness of snow and night. Instantly, the house went dark.

~

Elliot stood solemnly in his door. "No tickee, no partee."

"Chili," Ebie said, and held up our contribution.

"Already in a foil pan," I added, "to go straight on the grill."

"It's the original loaves and fishes party," Elliot had said that morning when the entire block woke to dim and chilly homes: no coffee, no television, no heat. "Bring a bottle, a friend, and whatever's thawing in your freezer."

Russ and Ebie and I had walked over, aiming for the ice-free patches of pavement exposed by a few hours of sunshine and determined drivers. Snow-blanketed and unelectrified, Liberty Ave was a monochromatic streetscape of pale blue-grays. Shouts of nighttime sledders blocks away were amplified in the eerie stillness, ringing out clearly as voices over water.

"I want to sled in the dark," Ebie said. "It sounds fun."

I entered Elliot's house half expecting to smell marijuana. The small room overflowed with folks outsized by extra clothing: some familiar faces, but more strangers, young people. Three men waved at me from across the room, and I stared for a moment, trying to place them. So did Russ. "Who are they?"

It came to me. "Elliot's crew." Mack, Flick, and Gus. Where was Diego?

Candles flickered on tables and windowsills and counters and shelves and even on the television set, bayberry and vanilla and clove-scented, multi-wicked, shaped in spirals and squares and spheres, tinted purple and green, some with fir branches and leaves and pine cones embedded in the wax.

"I could've brought my candle colored like a rainbow," Ebie said. She'd been delighted to be included in the party invitation, such as it was.

Elliot pointed his beer bottle at a slight boy wearing brown corduroys, lace-up boots and a V-necked rag sweater over a white T-shirt. "Jenny brought the fancy candles because the only thing in her freezer was ice cream."

The slight boy wasn't a boy after all. From across the room Jenny gave us a slow smile in a face made more elfin by her reddened nose and the close-fitting tightly-knit toboggan that covered her head. Nordic reindeer pranced across her brow, and braided tasseled ties dangled from the earflaps like Ebie's cornrows. *A friend*, I thought, and then suddenly, *or girlfriend*. Ebie was enchanted by the guests, the pierced nose here, the goatee there, Birkenstocks and leggings, men in bib overalls. My fascination was of a different sort. *He*

SUSAN KELLY

has a life, I thought, watching Jenny; *a life I know nothing of and don't belong to. He isn't exclusively mine any more than Bett is exclusively Ebie's.*

"Quite a crowd," Russ said.

"Cabin fever brings out the diversity," Elliot grinned, "including the food. Last time I checked, bananas were roasting on the grill beside a batch of shrimp and something that I *think* was a chicken casserole."

"We're supposed to get electricity back any time now," Russ said.

Elliot leaned down and snatched Ebie. She squirmed, doubling up under his tickled attack. "You savage!" he growled as she fought him, laughing. "You mutilated my creations! Confess, you scoundrel! Where are my snowmen's noses?"

"No!" Ebie squealed. "They had plastic surgery, a nose job!"

"Tell!" Elliot demanded, digging his fingers into her armpits, squeezing the nape of her neck.

She laughed hysterically, helplessly. "Frostbite made them fall off! Squirrels stold them."

"Stole," I laughed as well, and staggered backward as Ebie escaped behind me, clutching my upper arms.

"Anything to drink?" Russ asked. I knew he'd scanned the room of moving, mingling bodies for Anne and Darrell.

"This way," Elliot said, "in my Martha Stewart icebox." We wound through the kitchen, dodging people talking and smoking and gesturing and sitting on counters amid open bags of chips and open cabinet doors.

Necks of every variety of bottle stuck from a bank conveniently formed by snow that had slid from the roof above Elliot's back stoop. Beers and sodas and wine, flavored vodkas and hard lemonade and liqueurs. Even a lemon and a lime were buried in the snow bank, a citrus still-life. A brandy bottle stood warming at the outer edges of one of two kettle grills chockablock with mixing bowls and sizzling meats and char-striped bread slices dripping grease and butter onto embered briquettes. They glowed redly, casting shadows that tinted snow blue and hovering faces pink.

"What are these?" Ebie asked Elliot, and pointed to a pair of flat blackened trays stuck upright in the snow bank.

"Meany Matheny's cookie sheets," Elliot said. "But tonight they're sleds."

Ebie clapped her hands, delighted with the improvisation and transfixed by it all.

And it *was* a happy scene, infinitely more joyful than another party—complete with candles and liquor and pot luck—of six months ago in September. Such a difference. Was it the youthful guests and their bedraggled, casual appearance? Or was it the snow, the holiday air, the impromptu camaraderie? Perhaps it was only me, a different Laura from that sad, suffering person sleep-walking with grief. A recovered Laura.

At last granted access to the mysteries of Meany Matheny's off-limits property, Ebie was exploring the bark-sided smokehouse on stilts at the edge of her backyard. Whit had been fascinated by the primitive little cabin with its single window and ladder to the door. It fulfilled every Daniel Boone and Boxcar Children fantasy a child harbors, and tonight it looked appealing rather than neglected, snug and nestled and protected, six feet above the snow.

Acrid smoke filled the crisp night air, and I saw Russ accept a thick cigar from someone. He'd found his Labor Day friends. I wandered inside, smiled as one guest carefully created a crème de menthe snow cone while another flavored hers with Kahlúa. Melted wax spilled from the lip of a candle on the cluttered counter and I dipped a finger into the hot greasy puddle.

"What's this?" someone with a beard said beside me, and pulled a tiny flashlight key chain from his pocket.

He directed the flashlight beam on a flecked whitish mixture, gave the dip a dubious look, and turned away. But I was struck not by the contents but by the container: a french onion soup bowl. The heavy crockery bore handle stubs, and was fired a rich glazed brown with pale edges, as though cheese had melted and dripped. The sight of it pierced me with bittersweet sentiment. I owned six of those homely, homey soup bowls myself, proudly purchased for my first apartment though I'd needed pots and pans more urgently. Possessing the bowls *signified* something: romantic dinners for two on winter evenings with wine and candlelight and meaningful intimate looks. Years passed and though I'd never cooked onion soup even once, I couldn't part with what those crocks—grown dusty with age—represented. So I'd put them in the attic thinking, *Whit will want these one day.*

I touched the bulging bowl reflecting candlelight. Perhaps Elliot hadn't bought it; perhaps his mother had discovered her set in the attic, too, saved there for her son's future.

I stuck a finger into the sauce, tasted. Storebought onion dip, a concoction I gobbled and craved as a teenager but hadn't eaten in twenty years.

Someone poked me in the ribs. I looked up into the mask of a rapist or serial killer, a full-head ski stocking, the eye and mouth holes rimmed in red and black, odd objects sticking between the lips. But I recognized the corroded buttons on the plaid shirtfront, and was struck with affection for his inept ironing abilities. *Teach me to iron,* Whit had said once. *Placket last,* I'd said. *What's a placket?* he'd asked.

"Boo," he managed around his mouthful.

"You look like a criminal."

"And you have red wine teeth."

I covered my mouth and reddened, but felt a warm pleasure that he'd noticed. "What's in your mouth?"

Elliot stripped off the mask and his curls sprang wildly up. "Grilled shrimp. Nobody told me you had to take off the fins." He pulled them out like toothpicks and I thought of Whit in the stroller, leaf stems in his lips.

"The only liquor you can taste through a cold is gin because it burns your tongue," someone assuredly informed Jenny, who was standing nearby wiping her nose.

I talked to Mack and Gus, met a web page designer with seven barrettes in her hair, and a PhD student in Religious Studies who insisted on showing me a card trick by candlelight. The noisy party showed signs of extending well past Ebie's bedtime, regardless of no school again the next day, and I stood on tiptoes against the spindly makeshift bookshelves to scan the boisterous crowd for her. Someone brushed by and knocked me against a fraying catchall wicker basket filled with old magazines and sports gear—a baseball glove, the webby pocket of a lacrosse stick—an extension cord, DVDs. I leaned to read the titles—*A River Runs Through It, Dumb and Dumber*—and glimpsed what looked like a miniature Christmas stocking knitted in green and red and white yarn. Except that . . . I plucked it from beneath a dog-eared Michael Crichton paperback and examined the gaily striped pouch more closely.

I'd seen one before, but like the onion dip, not in two decades. It had floated around my sorority house the weeks before Christmas, been pinned to the message board or stashed in some unsuspecting sister's mail cubby. A gag gift waiting to be claimed or passed on. If there was a more precise or technical name for what I was holding, I didn't know it. It was a cock sock, complete with braided ties at the opening like the tasseled cords on Jenny's toboggan. Was this her Christmas present to Elliot, this dick warmer?

I spied her across the room, pictured her laughing as Elliot opened the gift, pictured them—I pushed away the thought and made myself laugh instead. "I didn't realize you were a knitter," I'd say to Jenny when I next saw her.

With a slight *pop*, the room burst into light and I instantly, guiltily, dropped the dick warmer. Cheers and boos rose from the jolly crowd blinking like woken children.

"House lights up!"

"Where was Moses when the lights went on?"

"In a blaze of glory!"

"Free at last, free at last!" someone crowed, and squatting before Elliot's sound system, boomed music into the room. Dave Matthews, one of Whit's favorite bands. He'd bragged that the group had performed at a Windsor Spring Formal before his time, when they were nobodies accepting any gig they were offered.

I made my way through moving bodies to Mack. "Have you seen my daughter?"

"Short person?" he grinned. "Not wearing a hat?"

"That's the one," I laughed.

"She's skitching with Elliot."

"Skitching? What's that?"

Mack gave me a look of mock astonishment. "You've never skitched? What a sheltered life you lead. Never skitched, never taken down a tree."

The front door banged open and a girl in a red parka stood on tiptoe scanning the crowd. "Is Laura in here anywhere?"

"Me," I said, trying to raise my voice to be heard.

"Over here," Mack called, hand on my shoulder.

Spotting me, the girl gestured frantically, her mouth a hard line. With knotted stomach I pushed through the rowdy crowd to reach her across the snow-wet floor cluttered with discarded cups and shed jackets. "Are you Evie's mother?" she asked with anxious eyes.

"Ebie—" Fear pinched my voice. "Where is she?"

But she'd already turned, words whipping over her shoulder. "An accident."

Slipping and skidding on the icy driveway, falling once, I ran behind her toward a car's high beams, twin searchlights in the middle of the street four houses down.

"Mack!" I screamed at the black figure silhouetted in the open door, "Find Russ! My husband!"

Crouched figures were shadows inside an exhaust cloud billowing from a pickup's tailpipe, but none of the apparitions was small enough to be Ebie. My heart banged, racing in my ribcage with panting and panic. My Ebie. My baby. My only baby. Not again. Not another mangled child. Not another Whit. *"Ebie!"*

She was a dark, still shape on a white surface. Her face and forehead were scraped and bleeding, and her right arm was twisted sickeningly above her head. So still. So deathly, deathly still. I thought I might pass out, or vomit, and dropped to my knees beside her.

"She's unconscious," someone said. "Help me lift her."

I knew that voice. Elliot. "What have you done to her?"

"I had her by the armpits, and—"

"Don't you touch her!"

"Laura, let me—"

I cradled her head in one arm and tried to lift the dead weight of her legs with the other. Ebie, Ebie. "Talk to me, Ebie."

"He was holding on to her the whole time," someone said, "but the sheet hit a storm drain so they pitched forward and—"

Then I saw the rope tied to the truck's boat hitch, the flat blackened cookie sheet, the storm drain where snow and ice had melted, leaving a perfect circle of rough grid in a street where tires had left gaps in the snow as well. Saw Elliot Hatcher skitching with my child on a flimsy cookie sheet behind an automobile and saw the sudden stop and jolt as the makeshift sled hit the bare metal, saw Ebie thrown forward and down and—"You—"

Elliot's pupils were bright pinpoints in the light. "Let me—"

I silenced him with a look. "Get her in the car, the truck, whatever it is," I said to the stranger. "Take us to the hospital, go!" The driver lifted Ebie onto the cracked seat of the truck cab and I knelt again beside her, mindless of the sharp twitch in my back bent beneath the dash. "Ebie," I whispered. "It will be all right."

Her eyes fluttered open. "Mom," she whimpered.

Relief flooded through me. "I'm here, honey. We're going to the hospital."

Her eyes squeezed shut and tears coursed down

her brow and into her ears. "My arm hurts," she cried, "so bad."

The pain in her voice, her helplessness, torqued my heart. "Hold on, sweetie."

The stranger shifted gears and eased the truck down an icy incline. All over the neighborhood, houses were shining with electricity, safe and restored. Not Ebie, not my baby. I gently touched her raw bleeding cheek, then lifted my eyes. I didn't look at the driver, didn't even ask his name. What I saw was my hurt child, the only child left to me, and the tow rope snaking behind the truck, and a single figure growing smaller in the street. Elliot. Elliot had done this.

"I want to see her."

I'd been calm, helpful, controlled; had answered questions and filled out forms and given a history and gritted my teeth when she shrieked during the X-ray, grateful for the small gift that she was conscious to scream in pain. I tried to explain so she could understand what had happened, and what was going to happen. Russ had been even quieter, and with Ebie safely in capable hands, I sensed his anger, feared it. We'd each held a hand and assured her all was fine as the anesthesia took hold. It seemed hours ago.

"She'll be asleep a good while," the orthopedist said. "It was a bad break. The pin is just above the elbow." He massaged the back of his neck.

"She was unconscious—"

"Slight concussion, according to the admitting doc," he said. "That'll be monitored too." Nurses passed us in the hall. The emergency room had been chaotic with injured, waiting patients. "It's always nuts when it snows. Brings out the crazies. What was she doing, again?"

"She was—" *Not she, no. They. He. Elliot. Elliot's fault.* "They were sledding behind a car."

The surgeon shook his head wearily. "Kids," he said, "think they're immortal."

I pressed my fist to my lips, and Russ's fingers tightened on my arm. "And the cuts?"

"Superficial abrasions. You can call a plastic surgeon if you like but I don't think that's necessary. Ought to heal just fine." He glanced at a clock overhead. "The arm will take a good eight weeks though, even at her age."

"I'm staying the night."

"Probably a good idea," the doctor said. "You're lucky. Snow may bring out the crazies, but they're mostly treat and release. She'll have a nice room for her short stay."

Lucky, I thought. *Lucky.*

"There's no extra bed but the window seat has a kind of mattress," he went on, setting the clipboard on the counter. "She's still in recovery but you can sit with her."

"I'll go home and get you some clothes and your toothbrush," Russ said.

"Thank you," I said, and kissed him. To Dr. Andrews I said, "Please take me."

The recovery area was a large, open, windowless room behind double doors that sighed open automatically. Rolling carts of monitors and medical supplies stood about like islands. The equipment—steel bed rails and metal housing of fluorescent lights and cabinets, even the pale green linoleum floor and pale blue walls—lent the room a chilly, sterile air. Ebie was the only patient in one of the half-dozen beds jutting perpendicular to the wall.

She was such a small figure in the wide white bed cranked higher than my waist; so pale beneath the gauze squares and adhesive tape on her face, beneath the sickly, relentless hospital light. The bulky cast stretched from shoulder to thumb, chalky and dry and heavy as concrete.

A spasm of gratitude made me tremble. Because she would be alright. She would wake and she would hurt and her face would scab and her head would throb and she wouldn't be able to write or play the piano or ride her bike for eight weeks. But she would live; I wouldn't lose her. She'd never even been near to ... to Whit. *Lucky*, Dr. Andrews had said. So lucky. She might have hit her head on the pavement instead of her arm, and injured her brain, her spinal cord; might have been left paralyzed, or speechless. She might have slid beneath the truck, been trapped or crushed by rolling tires and a ton of automobile—

There was neither name nor description for such unimaginable despair.

The lines rose from nowhere, stored deep in my brain since a sixth grade memorization assignment, whole verses of an ineffably sad elegy for a dead child, a father's thoughts while he watched falling snowflakes together with the only child left him.

> *The snow had begun in the gloaming,*
> *And busily all the night*
> *Had been heaping fields and highways*
> *With a silence deep and white.*
>
> *I thought of a mound in sweet Auburn*
> *Where a little headstone stood;*
> *How the flakes were folding it gently,*
> *As did robins the babes in the wood.*
>
> *Again I looked at the snow-fall,*
> *And thought of the leaden sky*
> *That arched o'er our first great sorrow,*
> *When that mound was heaped so high.*
>
> *I remembered that gradual patience*
> *That fell from that cloud like snow,*

Flake by flake, healing and hiding
The scar that renewed our woe.

Then, with eyes that saw not, I kissed her;
And she, kissing back, could not know
That my *kiss was given to her sister,*
Folded close under deepening snow.

I kissed my living child, too, the flannelly cheeks, the tiny veins pulsing bluely on her eyelids. Warm, breathing, only asleep. I went to wash my face and meet Russ and return before she stirred. She'd wake, and I'd be here.

He was walking toward me from the nurse's station, his untucked shirttail a flapping green and white triangle against his jeans. "Is Ebie okay? Where is she?"

She'd asked that just before they put her under. "Is Elliot okay? Where is he?" I hadn't answered.

I looked at Elliot's abraded face and cut lip and worried eyes. Shoestrings trailed behind him and I was reminded of the rope that jerked behind the truck on the way to the hospital. I stared at the misshapen shirt buttons and couldn't believe I'd ever found them poignant, couldn't believe I'd laughed with Elliot Hatcher, or defended him, or trusted him. Exhaustion and anxiety curdled into deadly outrage as I breathed and watched and blamed him. "Why are you here? How dare you come."

"I was worried, so—"

"Who do you think you are?"

"I shouldn't have let—"

"You know *nothing* of losing someone, *nothing.*" All the long bleak days of dumb bewildered misery, the nights when sadness was blacker than the night, rushed back to envelop me in the glaring brightness of the hospital hall. Everything my son had said, every object in his room, the final, forever and ever *goneness* of Whit fed the blame. "What gall you have, what arrogance! Take chances with your own life but not someone who belongs to *me*," I said cruelly to Elliot, knowing even as I flung the accusations that Ebie had begged to go with him, that she'd pleaded to be included in his fun, that his arms had been crossed over her chest and that she'd held tight to them. That what had happened was purely an accident, nothing more. "What were you *think*ing?"

"Laura. Please."

"How did you get up here?"

"I said I was related to Ebie. Is she—"

"You were not thinking *anything,*" I interrupted, "and you are *not* related to her. You're *nothing.* The last thing either of us needs is you." I pivoted so sharply that the boots' rubber treads squealed on the linoleum. The boots I was wearing were Whit's boots. "Go away, Elliot."

Chapter Thirteen

SHE COULDN'T UNDERSTAND WHY HE DIDN'T COME TO VISIT her, or even answer his door. "You yelled at him, Mom, didn't you? You spazzed out."

"He shouldn't have taken you skitching. It was dangerous." I looked at an icicle hanging from the eave, a crystal dagger growing shorter and sharper with every hour. "Besides, I expect he's busy. Ice does a lot of damage to trees."

Ebie wedged the letter opener into the cast at the palm opening.

"Don't do that, you might break the skin."

"It itches worse than the hat. I liked Jenny's toboggan, didn't you? Remember Jenny at Elliot's party?"

I remembered. Remembered the toboggan. Remembered the dick warmer. Remembered Elliot's concern at the hospital. Remembered denouncing and accusing and rejecting him. And now I regretted what I'd done.

"Jenny was nice," Ebie said.

I remembered as well what I'd felt about Jenny: disapproval. Disappointment. And one emotion I didn't want to examine: jealousy.

"Jenny has every Disney video and she's, like, *old.*"

Ah. So she was the friend he'd mentioned the day we met, in October.

"Jenny said I should play 'Tender Shepherd' for my recital piece and it's not even Disney." Ebie plinked a three-fingered tune on the piano keys.

I fidgeted at the window. Melting ice is like rain in sunlight, a peculiar visual of water streaming from a roof even as the sun shines overhead. But it's the *noise* that drives you mad, the steady rhythmic *lup lup lup lup lup*, as though a dog is ceaselessly lapping water.

"Do you think Jenny is Elliot's girlfriend?" Ebie asked.

I watched the dripping leave pockmarks on the fretwork of porous snow still clinging to the shade of the house's foundations. "That boy is being wasted," Anne had said in early January. "Why don't you get him a date, set him up with someone?" It was a reasonable suggestion, even an obvious one, but I'd never moved on it, stalled by undiagnosed feelings. Suppose the setup didn't work out? Then Elliot might compare the girl to me, since she was my choice for him, and think less of me. But beneath this unattractive logic was something darker: I didn't want Elliot's relationship with, or affection for me, to be diminished or compromised by someone else. A selfish reason and not a healthy one, that revealed something, I understood even then that I wouldn't want anyone to know. And that was dangerous.

"How about a game?" I answered Ebie instead, and stared at marshy spots in the low-lying areas of the yard. "Crossfire?"

"I have homework. And I can't shoot with my cast." Ebie lifted her thick, useless arm. "Besides, it wouldn't be as much fun without . . ." She trailed off, then brightened. "I know. You're doing to Elliot what you told me to do to Bett. 'Playing it cool.'" She giggled, entertained by an obsolete phrase and her deduction.

I dragged my eyes away from the window shade beyond the fence, closed now, as though Meany Matheny still lived there. "Watching isn't a neutral activity," he'd told me. A poplar branch shone wetly bare when only yesterday it had been coated, winking in the sun.

"I miss Elliot," Ebie said. Straightforward and honest with herself, unlike her mother. "Don't you?"

Miss him? *You won't be able to actually see it happen,* I'd warned Ebie about the falling thermometer.

It happens that fast, or that gradually. Which? Is a slippery slope, a gradual incline, or a steep tilt?

Soiled mountains of plowed snow dotted the medical complex parking lot like slag heaps, the only remaining evidence of March's storm.

"Coming along fine," Dr. Andrews had told Ebie during the check-up. "You'll be ready for baseball season."

She'd hopped down from the examining table and informed him, "I play the piano, not baseball."

I eased the car over a hummock of stubborn ice as high as the lot's speed bumps. "Do you think Elliot will come to my recital in May?" Ebie asked. "Where *is* he? It's like he's hiding from us."

Salt had left telltale ashy smears on cars and collected at curbs like Styrofoam pellets, harsh contrasts to the soft mounds of dropped dogwood petals that would bloom before long. We passed a yard littered with objects—a carrot, a hockey stick, ski goggles—around a solitary white mound on the muddied, flattened grass.

"Dead snowman," Ebie said, "like the wicked witch in *The Wizard of Oz*. 'I'm melting, I'm *mellllting!*'" she mimicked, high-pitched and shrill and dead-on. I flinched.

Another yard, another irregular lump listing

drunkenly. "Another dead snowman," Ebie said again.

I sighed. "Snow vanishes overnight if you live in Camelot."

"Where's that?"

"Never mind." We passed another sagging, collapsing white clump. Yard by yard, Ebie ticked them off in a bored monotone.

"Dying snowman."

"Unidentified blob. Dead snowman."

"Near-dead snowman."

"Stop that!" I snapped.

Stung by my harsh tone, her head whipped round from the window.

"It's just that . . ." I tried.

It's just that without Elliot I was shrinking again, too, receding like the snow and creeping bit by bit into thoughts of Whit and those shattered shuttered days filled with nothing but memories and misery. Six shrunken white stumps still sat on our lawn, and if Ebie were to drone six times, "Dead snowman, dead snowman, dead—" I myself would dissolve, from missing Whit and banishing Elliot.

"Your saying that makes me sad," I tried, part explanation, part apology. I was terrified of falling apart again, of returning to a crippled, tractionless indoor life of watching, not being.

"Oh," Ebie said, giving me a worried glance. She

remembered those days as well. "The igloo is gone, too," she said hopefully.

We passed the corner lot delineated now with foundation cinderblocks. A blue Port-O-Let stood where the chunks of sidewalks once had. Hillocks of ginger sand, leftovers from concrete mixing, stood like misplaced beach dunes. Tarps covered pallets of lumber. Framing would come next. I dreaded the sight as much as I dreaded passing Elliot's house and coming upon the six dying snowmen in our yard.

"Look!" Ebie shrieked.

I looked, and what a sight it was: a sudden, glorious, incredible vision forever imprinted on my memory.

White paper streamers cascaded from high, high in the poplar tree branches all the way to the earth. Thick as a beaded curtain, as though you'd part them to pass through, yet sheer and graceful and weightless, impossibly long and unbroken.

Ebie bounded out of the car, but I sat transfixed by the beauty of white descending to green lawn. They were ribbons ironed to limpness, uniform lengths that neither drooped nor fluttered in the afternoon stillness but hung suspended and weightless as dust motes. Our yard seemed a stage decorated for a ballet dream sequence, or an intentional work of art planned with no less care than Christo's sheet-wrapped fences and fields.

Ebie ran through the thin paper stripes. They draped her hair and shoulders, caressed her face, moved slightly with her movements. She seemed a woodland sprite flitting through an enchanted forest. My happy daughter, who'd always longed for the celebrity status bestowed by being the target of a roll job. "Getting rolled isn't a cut," she'd once solemnly informed me, "it's a compliment."

"We got rolled!" she trilled now, breaking the silent spell. "I've *always always* wanted to get rolled. Bett did it! She said she had a get-well present and she never brought it to me!"

Ebie was as certain of the perpetrator's identity as I was.

No child or teenager or even an adult with a strong pitching arm could achieve such maypole prettiness and perfection, leave no unused rolls of toilet paper behind, no broken bits or trod-upon pieces. This was more than stunt, more than random tossing. This creation had taken deliberation and orchestration. Only someone who knew trees could have created such a scene. Only someone at home with rooftop heights, who understood weight-bearing branches. Only someone with access to ladders and the biggest slingshot in the world.

I gazed at the theatrical sight, drinking in its accidental beauty. *Lovely,* he'd said that day as I sat on his car hood and watched the tall tree tossing its leafy head. That feminine word from that masculine mouth hadn't seemed strange at all.

Ebie had vowed that her rainbow-striped candle was too pretty to ever use, but it was half burned now, the violet lip curling backward from the black wick. If Elliot could burn candles, so would she. I pried hardened wax from the bathroom counter with my fingernail. "Is imitation the greatest form of flattery?"

"What?" she called from inside the closet where she was putting on her nightgown.

"What?" Russ echoed from Ebie's bedroom, surveying the water stains on the ceiling left by ice damming. He shook his head. "'Night, Ebes," he said to the closet door. "I'll get a painter over here."

The rug below Ebie's dry-erase whiteboard wall calendar was littered with wadded tissues smeared red and green and black, still smelling faintly of the markers' chemical ink. **MONTHLY GOALS** Ebie had listed in bold red printing on the calendar's margins.

> *Jog once a week.*
> *Good grades.*
> *Fifteen minutes pleasure reading a day.*
> *Less time on instant messenger and more time*
>   *outside.*

On the blank square blocks of days, she'd penned reminders to herself.

> *church youth group 5:30–7:30*
> *mythology test*
> *soccer 6–7:30*
> *piano*
> *piano*
> *piano*

Ebie climbed into bed and said, "I *like* the stain on the ceiling. It looks like a rabbit, like in *Madeline*." She arranged her heavy arm on an extra pillow. "I can't ever decide whether I want to be an orphan like Madeline since Whit's gone—"

"You are *not* an orphan."

"—or Eloise, '*me, Eloise*,'" she said, quoting the favorite story. "Maybe I'll just be Heebie Jeebie Ebie. That's what Elliot calls me."

I leaned to switch off the lamp. "Don't be mad at him, Mom." She giggled. "Bett says I have a crush on him."

Darkness is good for confession.

I lay awake though Russ had long since fallen asleep. Since, as a matter of fact, seconds after he'd rolled away from me. He could have complained or scolded, as he had that wretched September night of the pot-luck party: "You only get out of something what you put into it." Or he could have asked what was wrong with our love-making, though I couldn't have named a reason. But he'd done neither.

"Of course not," Anne once concluded with roll-eyed weariness, "Because they *always* come."

I tried to think of Anne, how I'd respond when she asked why I'd been avoiding her—and she was bound to ask, blunt Anne. The dilemma made me tired, but not sleepy. My hand traveled down between my legs, but it was too little too late.

Lup lup lup lup lup. Even at night, ice melts. I tossed, stared into the darkness, turned over. You'd be amazed at the number of birds awake at two in the morning. Finally I slipped from the covers and padded downstairs in moonlight so bright that its reflection on the glossy sansanqua leaves outside made the shrub look as though it was decorated with tiny white Christmas lights.

But no, there was only a soft-edged moon beyond the living room bay window. I mistook its brightness for the beam of Meany Matheny's back-yard streetlight, which Elliot had switched on tonight. I turned on the television, where talking heads brayed at each other. Maybe a movie would make me sleepy. I pushed PLAY on the DVD player and it whirred into life.

Into *life* . . .

I should have stopped it. Should not have backed slowly away and sat down, caught and hypnotized, on the sofa. Should have ejected the disc from its slot, should have seen HOME MOVIES hand-printed on the label. Watching Ebie strut and prance and lip-sync in imitation of seventeen-year-old nymphets on MTV would have pained me, but not in the way that what I watched pained me. Whit careened down a yellow Slip 'n Slide in the backyard holding a baby Ebie between his legs. Ten years old, the summer we'd bought the video camera. My inexperience with the zooming button jerked his face drunkenly close. Enlarged and distorted, it filled the screen. But every pore was precious to me.

He hung by one arm from the park jungle gym. Ten, again. He rolled his eyes into their sockets and stood among my tulips for an Easter picture. Eleven. He scowled from left field, presumably at the batter, then dropped his mitt to pick a four-leaf clover from the ground as the camera shook with my laughter. Twelve. He smiled at the stringy seeded Halloween pumpkin pulp squeezing between his fingers, a knife between his teeth, Indiana Jones style. Fourteen. He sat cross-legged before the fire, carefully cleaning a shotgun too new to need cleaning. Eighteen.

On and on, rewound and fast-forwarded. Not single photographs frozen forever but long minutes of him moving, batting, carving, swimming, eating, unwrapping, *living.* Until that beautiful, gift-from-God, living-right, day of graduation. There was my boy striding toward the podium, accepting his diploma, shaking the outstretched hand, and turning to flash that gone gone smile at us. The smile, the boy, forever gone.

Books and movies are wrong. You don't replay the accident a million times, ceaselessly turning that day and that event over and over in your mind. What you replay are all the sweet small inconsequential moments of a life.

I turned off the machine. When parents look at pictures of the smiling faces of their children as youngsters, they say *Oh, I could cry, I miss those days.* But what they really long for is that time when they didn't know what they know now. Not that there's been a particular tragedy, not that they, or life, was more innocent then, but that they just didn't *know.* Which is why people can't be speaking the truth when they say they'd like to see into the future.

I climbed the stairs and went into his room and softly shut the door and switched on the light and looked up at them: stars and moons and planets and comets and mere dots of distant suns or solar systems.

"Private sky," the packages were titled—or was that simply Whit's name for them?—that began as special-occasion gifts. Adhesive-backed, pale green glow-in-the-dark plastic, the color of Daiquiri Ice at

Baskin-Robbins. With time the planetary peel-offs were reduced to birthday party favors, and then further demoted to good-behavior handouts at school. Finally the stickers had become ubiquitous and ordinary, or he'd aged beyond them, or the fad had ended.

He'd plastered them randomly across his bedroom ceiling, a single star here, a cluster of comets there, even a celestial smiley face: star eyes, dot nose, a quarter moon for a grin. I turned off the light and lay down on his bed and watched them.

"How do you think he decided what to put where?" I'd asked Russ during that week-long trance after the funeral. I'd needed to know if Whit had meant to create something specific with the stickers—a horse, a Big Dipper, a wagon. "And why these two places, over the bed and in the corner near the bookshelves?" I'd yearned for the impossible: to know Whit's train of thoughts. To have him back.

"Probably because he could stand on the headboard and because he could stand on the chair beside the bookshelf to get them up there," Russ had answered. "Aren't you obsessing a bit?"

Oh, Russ. So logical, so reasonable. Yes, I suppose I was.

Like falling leaves and melting ice and kinds of love, the transition was almost undetectable. No matter how long a light is on, the sticky stars can absorb only a finite amount of light to return. No matter the size of the planet or star, they glow and then fade, almost as one, and the room became fully dark once again. I turned on the light, checked my watch. Twenty-two minutes of glowing comfort before I was left sleepless and alone again.

I thought of Ebie's calendar notations in her curling or shaded or blocky print, the thick exclamation points, the illustrations of soccer balls. Imagined her delight in penning the self-important reminders, her thrill in personal responsibility and pride in organization. Trivial scribbles easily erased with a single tissue. Meaningless details of a life—no different than Elliot's warped shirt buttons—that to someone else become meaningful, and more: poignant, cherished. How he'd sung "House at Pooh Corner" over and over at twelve; how I'd sung "My Best Beau" from *Mame* to him when I rocked him as a baby.

I sat up and switched on the light and stood on the bed and, one by one, peeled away my boy's private sky. Faint outlines were left on the ceiling as though someone had moved out, moved on. As had Whit, in a way, and I myself. Left behind were pale patches no different from the rectangles behind removed pictures on the walls of the tear-down house on the corner.

Russ slept on as I searched among shaving cream and shampoo bottles beneath the sink for a tiny felted bag. At last I found the drawstring pouch that had once been home to a ruby pin of my mother's and now held the last of two dozen sleeping pills prescribed for me after Whit's death that I'd carefully rationed.

But the final hoarded tablet was pulverized, crushed to dust by heavy soap bundles or extra toothpaste boxes. Oh, no. Please, please. I carefully, desperately, turned the pouch inside out and licked every trace of powder from the furry fabric. Please put me to sleep. Please let me go.

The dream came from nowhere. Vivid, detailed, without preamble.

A small attic room was angled under a slanted, tongue-and-groove, pastel-painted ceiling of a beach cottage. A catalog cottage to display summery linens and duvets and pillows. The billowy bed was there, the striped throw rug on the floor was there, the Queen Anne's lace in a glass jar on the windowsill was there, the flowy curtains letting in a rich afternoon light. All there.

And sex was there, too, on that catalog bed: intense, mute, writhing screwing. Elemental, explicit sex. Flailing limbs and arching torsos, bucking hips. Fingers whitened on backs, gripping the headboard, the mattress edge.

Then it was evening, with pale green artichokes on white crockery plates, frosted tumblers of blender drinks and a mesh basket of papayas. People I didn't seem to know meandered around the open kitchen, eating and talking. Except for him. Him, I knew. Yet he gave me nary a glance, much less a spoken greeting, to acknowledge we even knew each other, much less the afternoon of frantic, passionate love-making. Because along with the fierceness, the sensation that lingered was furtiveness.

I bolted up in bed, jolted from sleep not by a dream—an erotic vision that would stay with me all day and longer—but by a fever of arousal and desire so powerful I was breathing shallowly.

The clock read seven-thirty. Downstairs I heard Ebie asked Russ, "What's for breakfast?"

And I asked myself, When do friendship and affection evolve into, cross an invisible line into something else, something nearly unnamable? *What is it with you and Elliot Hatcher?* Russ had asked me

It was this: I was mad, I was hurt, I was jealous. And I was in love with the man of my dream. The man was the boy next door.

Chapter Fourteen

From Whit's window I saw Anne, though it wasn't like her to walk alone. I'd been a poor friend to her since the February evening when Russ told me of Darrell's decision to leave Lucas Con. Since he'd told me about Darrell and Sherry's probable affair. I was stymied by indecision, unsure of my role in a classic case of The Best Friend Who Knows.

"Am I obligated to tell her, or is it none of my business?" I'd worried to Russ. "I'm in the middle, loving both of them."

Now I cowardly ducked out of sight, hoping Anne would stroll on. Instead, she turned onto our front walk, and I surveyed my options.

If Anne had discovered Darrell's infidelity, there'd be justifiable rage or grief, and I'd agree and sympathize and console. If she'd discovered my prior knowledge, there'd be justifiable hostility and accusation and I'd be guilty and apologetic. And beyond those thorny issues was Darrell's departure from Lucas Con. A separation that nagged at me, despite Russ's explanation; a decision that seemed unfinished and abrupt and too . . . simple.

"Darrell's leaving is the end of something," I'd mused aloud to him. "A kind of innocence, maybe, as we knew it, as you and Darrell created it."

"Innocence?" Russ had echoed. "Don't be maudlin. This is a business. It's merely a different relationship. I'm thinking of a new name since all the stationery has to be changed anyway."

"Nothing will ever be the same between the four of us again," I'd said, groping to convey my feelings. "It's all . . . altered."

Expectant and anxious on several fronts, I beat Anne to the kitchen door with small talk on my lips. "Happy spring," I said. "The weeping willow's out. It's official."

Anne stepped inside. "Pear trees are first."

"First to blossom, not leaf. Bradford pears don't count." *Lined up like spades on a playing card*, he'd scoffed and I'd agreed that October day.

Anne eyed me. "You and your trees. Am I interrupting anything?"

"I'm . . ." What I was doing was meant to be a surprise for Russ. "I'm cleaning out Whit's room." *Sitting-around-stuff* Elliot had called it. I'd begun more than two weeks ago, in a way, with the ceiling stars that night of the erotic and uneasy dream. "Finally," I added.

Anne's features softened.

"It was never a shrine, but I just couldn't . . . I was just sad for so long. Now I can face it. Now that I'm . . . well."

Then the earlier, harder expression reappeared on Anne's face and I steeled myself for the inevitable. Poor Anne. How had Darrell told her? How had she found out? "Come on," I said. "We'll talk while I work." Anne followed me upstairs. Shopping bags filled with sweaters and pants and shirts lined the wall of Whit's room. "For Goodwill," I said.

"Adele went to Goodwill one time for T-shirts and came home with four that had 'Lucas' stamped on the collar," Anne said.

I smiled. "He had plenty to spare."

Anne put her hands in the rear pockets of her jeans. "Adele always loved Whit. Since playgroup days."

Whit had loved Adele as well, but not equally. As he packed to return to Windsor after his senior year spring break, Whit confessed, "I think Adele wanted to invite me to the Page prom, but I . . ."

"Made sure she didn't have an opportunity to ask?" I'd supplied, intuiting.

He flipped through a stack of SAT vocabulary practice words. "Yeah. Is that jerky?"

"A little."

"I just want, I don't know . . ."

"Not to be seen as hers alone?"

"Something like that, I guess. But it makes me feel bad that you agreed it was jerky."

"I was just being honest." I smiled, handed him a box of laundry detergent—that he'd never open—to take back to Windsor. "If I feel badly about something it's usually guilt, and I usually feel guilty because I've done something not necessarily bad, but not good."

"Laura . . ." Anne said now.

Edgy, and dreading a stunted, evasive conversation, I looked out the window. Below, shrubs still bore the effects of a foot of snow, splayed and gaping where they should have been bushy and full. "I'm afraid the boxwoods will never recover."

"Laura," Anne said again.

I waited, my back to her.

"You should know, Laura. People are *talking*."

An inner alarm went off. This wasn't the conversation I was prepared for. "About what?" My fingernails paled with pressure on the mullions.

She pulled a piece of newsprint from her pocket. "This, for one thing."

I looked at it, a photograph of Elliot and me with our small army of snowmen. "That picture was on a full page of photos taken after the snowstorm," I said to Anne. "The newspaper people hung around our neighborhood all day. Cath Barnhardt's picture was on the same page. She was sledding. So was Tim Holland's, building an igloo."

"With their children," she added pointedly.

I turned to the bookshelves, the multiple mugs. "Need an extra pencil holder?"

"He rolled your house."

"Yes, he did. For Ebie, because of the accident. And Elliot knew she was dying to get rolled."

"It just looks . . . fishy."

My face pinked, though Anne was behind me. "Fishy? What does that mean, 'fishy'?"

"You know."

"I do not know."

"There's a rumor that you're—that you're having an affair with him."

My mouth went dry. "That is ridiculous, patently untrue." I forced myself to swivel and face her. "And *mean*."

"I'm not telling you that you've done anything *wrong*." Anne's gaze was both curious and penetrating. "I'm just telling you how it *looks*."

"Elliot Hatcher is my neighbor and my friend. What's between us is one hundred per cent platonic. Look how young he is!"

"Yes," Anne said evenly, "I have indeed."

God, but she was brave. Aggressive and bold. Years

ago she'd flagged me over on my way home from a doctor's appointment. Leaning into the open car window to chat, she caught sight of the gauze square in the crook of my arm resting on the steering wheel. "You pregnant?" she'd asked, pointing to the patch. I was, just.

"Right," I said. "I'm guilty of—what would the term be?—inner child infidelity? For making snowmen and playing Crossfire. It's not exactly hanky-panky. It's not even done in private."

Anne sat down on Whit's bed. "So you're not in love with him?"

I stiffened. My words to Whit mocked me: *When I feel badly about something it's usually guilt, and I usually feel guilty because I've done something not good—not necessarily bad—but not good.*

I took care not to sound defensive. "In love with him?" I forced a laugh. "It's so much *tamer* than that. You're as bad as Russ," I plunged on, "who says I'm replacing Whit with Elliot, that I'm attracted to him because of his hair." Instantly, I realized my mistake.

"*Attracted* to him? Laura, listen to the word you chose. Listen to what you even *say*, the way you phrase it."

How wrong I'd been, assuming Anne had sought me out because of her own problems. How the tables had turned. I mentally drew myself up. This could go no further.

"No, you listen to me, Anne. Not even a glance between us has been . . . improper." I hated the way I sounded, like a Jane Austen character. "As a matter of fact I haven't laid eyes on Elliot since the night of Ebie's accident. I've exiled him for his irresponsibility."

Anne leaned back on her elbows. "I just thought you'd like to know what the rumor is."

"Rumors," I said with disgust. "Remember the rumor that Jocelyn and Will Maxwell's weekend babysitter was having an affair with—?" I stopped, caught myself, but it was too late, again.

"—Will Maxwell?" Anne supplied, a smug chirp. "And she was."

"Rumors," I said again. Plainly, Anne knew nothing of her husband and Sherry Weaver. *Sometimes*, Russ had said hotly, *a rumor is as damaging as a fact*. My friend sat blithely secure in her ignorance, spouting nothing more than the latest neighborhood gossip.

"How long have we been dealing with rumors, Anne? Forever. Even Liberty Ave *real estate* is rife with tales. The rumor that this house sold for such-and-such, the rumor that so-and-so are splitting because they put their house on the market, the rumor that so-and-so's addition has a private screening room for porno flicks. The rumor that the house on the corner was torn down to make room for a French chateau with an English garden."

Anne stared. "Rumor?"

"Oh yes, haven't you *heard*?" I laughed in nosy old biddy imitation, relieved that the conversation had veered away from Elliot.

She seemed not to have heard me; slowly folded the square of newsprint. "I don't understand what's happened to Russ, what's made him so greedy, or aggressive." She shook her head. "It must be especially hard for you, feeling so strongly about this neighborhood, keeping it—its *integrity*—intact."

Confused, I frowned. What about the neighborhood? "Because of Darrell? Has he found another—"

"Darrell?" Anne interrupted. She leaned forward in a posture of concern and pinned me with a look. "You don't know, do you." Her voice was low. "You don't even know."

Suddenly I did, or believed I did. "Russ *did* fire Darrell, didn't he. Even though Russ said it was mutual. I felt it in my bones, *knew* it, damn him."

"Mutual?" Anne stared at me with both tender and condescending pity. "Fired? I supposed that's one way of looking at it. With me or agin me is the other way."

"What?"

"Darrell *chose* to leave Lucas Con because he refused to be involved in it."

"In what?"

Anne's sympathy became impatience. "Down the street. The razing, the double lot on the corner. It isn't a rumor, Laura. The French chateau and the English garden is Russ's project. *Russ's*."

I knelt and put the mug on the carpet, afraid my shaking fingers would drop it. *Sometimes a rumor is as damaging as a fact.*

"He didn't tell you?" Anne asked.

"He—" My armpits grew damp as I tried to remember what Russ had said. Or what he hadn't said.

I came home early because I was in the neighborhood . . . overseeing a crew . . . Darrell and I have developed different interests. We want the company to go in different directions . . . Darrell and I want different things, Laura, have different goals for the company. I'm thinking bigger, more long-term.

The reasons he'd given, the reasons he hadn't. Lies of omission and blatant lies as well.

"I thought you knew," Anne said softly, mingling comfort with superiority. "I'm sorry to be the one to . . . to tell you. And you're right about you and Elliot. It's just vicious gossip in a neighborhood with nothing but construction and house sales to talk about." She heard herself adding salt to a wound. "I mean—damn my candor, it keeps me in trouble." She stood and touched me solicitously on the shoulder. "I should go. Call me."

I delivered the bags to the Goodwill attendant in the open trailer and let Whit's belongings go without a pang. *Done*, I thought, the way Whit and all the Windsor students imitated a coach when the team scored: "Done!" I drove aimlessly, waiting for fury to descend, for the righteous anger that was surely due me. My husband had left his best friend and business partner no choice but to leave their company. My husband had the bigger bat so the game had to be played his way. My husband's bigger bat was a construction deal he'd kept secret from me. A project he knew I'd loathe on a street he knew I loved. I had multiple reasons for rage, for shouting, for confrontation. But instead of hot fury there was only heaviness, a heaviness I recognized: sorrow.

It will never be the same, I'd told Russ. *An innocence has been destroyed*, I'd said, *forever altered*. I'd meant our friendship with the McCalls, with no premonition that the words might apply, one day in the future, to the two of us.

Long before I ever reached the corner of Liberty Ave I slowed. The street was impassable. A crane spanned the pavement in order to lift a raw arch that I knew would become an entrance. An entrance so large it required a crane to install. I could envision the future house clearly now. The facade would be less than fifteen feet from the curb, normally a setback code violation. Russ, no doubt, had argued his case for the city council and won. He was persuasive, he had a good reputation as a builder, he was hardworking. And honest.

I parked behind trucks with indeterminate-purpose, subcontractor vehicles. Tall shrubbery on my right shielded the view. Except that it wasn't shrubbery but a veritable wall of sod, rolls of grass stacked five feet high, ready to be laid like carpet on the bare earth of an English-garden-to-be.

"You can't do that," Elliot had said that afternoon as we sat on the split rail fence. We were panting with exertion and puffed with satisfaction after ripping up the ivy. I was debating what to plant in the newly naked dirt, musing the benefits of an insta-yard. "Sodded grass is like underground sprinklers," Elliot had said. "It's cheating."

Now I noticed Russ's profile in the cab of a truck with a magnetized sign plate on the door. LuCon it read, with new font and new logo, snappy and authoritative. The "fresher name" he'd casually mentioned when I was struggling to decide what was best to tell, or not tell, Anne.

His head was bent over a clipboard. Building permits, I suspected, required to be posted on site. The secret project wouldn't be secret for long. My husband's secret, for which he'd razed a home, butchered a sidewalk, and sacrificed three gorgeous trees.

I watched Russ. We were in the same English

class one college semester, and I'd written two papers on the same Tom Stoppard play. One for me, one for Russ. Because I loved him so, I'd have done anything for him, including cheating. Including doing his laundry, needlepointing a backgammon board, borrowing a friend's car and taking dinners to him at the mall those evenings he clerked at the sporting goods store.

He introduced me to Aaron Copland while we studied at his apartment, music as wide and soaring and inspirational as the American West it represented: cowboys thundering across golden plains, billows of clouds and snow-capped mountains behind them.

Over Sunday-night pizza we speculated on the children we'd have, trying out names and gender combinations, predicting what kind of parents we'd be. I'd played along, caught up in the game, but all that mattered to me was what the conversation represented: that Russ felt secure enough of our future together to engage in such a committing dialogue.

I watched Russ a moment longer. How I'd loved him.

"I'm not one of those people who believe there's one person intended for them," I said once to Whit, "that there's only one soul mate in the world I was meant for, could be happy with."

"Nobody believes that," he'd returned.

"Girls do," I said. "You'd be surprised at the

number of girls who subscribe to the Prince Charming theory."

An unfamiliar car was parked in front of our house. I pulled into the driveway, walked around back, and found a woman in a business suit standing on the terrace taking pictures. "Can I help you?" I asked, unsure whether to be puzzled or alarmed.

"Oh," she said, bringing the camera down from her face. "I'm just finishing up."

"Finishing what?"

"Photographs are required for the appraisal."

"Appraisal for what?"

She shrugged. "Second mortgage, maybe? Sale listing? Beats me, I'm just a bank employee." She frowned slightly, as though she'd revealed too much to someone who had no business knowing hers. "Do you live here?"

"Yes."

"Then it's good you came home." She pointed to the mullioned door leading to the terrace. "Were you aware of this?" Two middle panes were broken. Glass shards were scattered on the bricks. "Look at that. Unbelievable what these druggies will do. And in broad daylight."

I stared, tying to imagine such desperation. The jagged glass edges in the broken pane were bloody.

"They broke the glass and stuck their wrist through trying to get to the door handle. Good thing it's dead-bolted. Good thing you weren't home, too. And I've always heard this was a *nice* neighborhood." She shook her head, looked dubiously at the rickety stilted smokehouse next door, its rusted tin roof. "Well, I'll push on so you can call the police."

She got in her car and drove away with her camera and her photographs. What was Russ doing now? Why was he having our home appraised? What new secret was he harboring? *Don't you want more?* he'd asked me.

Not at the expense of Darrell or at the expense of Winwood. Or at the expense of you and me, I should have said. Would have said, if I'd known the whole truth.

"You're so gullible," Russ had teased me in college, and I felt warm and complimented by his flirty affection. And the way I'd feel now, I admitted to myself, if Elliot were to say the same to me. But I'd severed Elliot with my harsh denunciations at the hospital, more than a month ago.

I swept up the pieces of glass and put them in the recycling bin. I checked my watch, remembered that Ebie was going home with Bett after school. I didn't call the police. Russ could do that. He wouldn't be home, not for hours.

A brilliant blue flashed by, so beautiful that I gasped. Unmistakably a bluebird, a rare winged creature in city limits among my ordinary sparrows and wrens and jays and even cardinals. That vivid but elusive color disappeared as swiftly as it had startled me.

Head in my hands, I sat on a terrace chair. *So many kinds of lies*, I thought; lies to others, to ourselves, omitted or outright. So many definitions of cheating. So many varieties of accidental villains, accidental betrayals, accidental endings. To neighborhoods, friends, marriages. Darrell to Anne, I to Anne, Russ to Darrell, Russ to me. And I to Elliot.

Elliot.

His eyes widened when he saw me standing beside the grill at his back door. "Are you home?" I asked.

He nodded.

"I'm sorry, Elliot, so sorry. I shouldn't have treated you the way I did. The way I have been."

"You were right to be furious. I'm sorry, too. I shouldn't have taken Ebie with me."

I gazed at him, the tiny dark freckles of scabs still left on his cheeks. At his curls and eyes and chin. Russ was wrong. Elliot was nothing at all like Whit. "I came to see you because . . ." *Ebie misses you*, I almost said. But—

No. No more lies. "I came because I miss you."

He reached for me and pulled me inside and shut the door behind us.

Chapter Fifteen

Here is what you think. You think—

Except that you're not thinking. Because you're doing. And being done to.

He unbuttons your shirt where your nipples are tingling and tightened, straining against bra lace. They want to be sucked, and you hold your breasts yourself, afraid you'll bodily buckle if he doesn't— but he does, reaches beneath to free them even as you reach behind to unclasp. He squeezes each nipple in the V of two fingers and unwittingly pulls as well on strands of hair falling forward because your head bends over in mute pleasure at the sensation and release of this double tugging. You press back, your flattened palms against the small tough nubs of his own nipples, and then, hooking your fingers in the belt loops of his jeans, you pull, too. Tug down, freeing him as he unzips and frees you, and somehow your mouths have locked while your clothing has puddled on the floor.

You think you'll be bashful with your body fourteen years older than his, because you're so fully naked and exposed as he kneels, lowering his lips and tongue from breasts to belly, lowering his hands and fingers from nipples to buttocks. You hold either side of his head, your pinkies in the small warm holes of his ears while your other fingers disappear into his wooly curls as his fingers tangle in the curls between your legs then gently part you and reach inside you, probe.

You think you'll be shy but there's no reticence, only response. You pant as your vagina contracts; it wants to grip something. It pulses and throbs and you think you'll lose consciousness if he doesn't—*Elliot!*—but he does, stands and reaches behind him for the bed and pulls you down with him.

He covers your mouth with his and covers your body with his and beneath him, you fit him, and with your legs wide your hands reach down, find his clenched buttocks. You palm the small concave hollows on either side, then reach around and down to his balls. Your touching startles him and he pulls away from your mouth, and smiling with surprised delight he rears above you, and you watch him while all you think is *Elliot, do me.*

He crouches over you and lifts your rump and

moves you back and forth, gently pushing into you; too-brief, too-shallow nudges as though patiently asking questions he knows the answer to—Like this? Like this?—and then sits back and pulls out while you nearly thrash and spread wider and beg with your eyes—please, please—until he begins the slow deep plunges that withhold his coming and prolong a form of exquisitely tender torture.

And when you have shuddered and caught your breath again he pulls you up by your wrists, and astride him, your knees at his hips. *Elliot, no,* you say wordlessly, shaking your head, sated and slaked. But he ducks his head and fastens his mouth to your breasts and fastens you to his groin and pushes inside you again. Face-to-face and upright, there is all the time in the world as you rock in a tantalizingly slow friction of belly to belly and chest to chest. You still slippery and full, he still hard as . . . as the boy he is.

"What are you doing at home during the day?"

He curled his bigger hand over my exploring one, warming my touch on his hip. "I'm off for good behavior, for working nonstop since the ice. Not just the damage that's already done, but with homeowners panicked about some branch or tree they just *know* will come through their roof and crush them. They want trees cabled, though I try to dissuade them because if a cabled tree goes down it takes down others with it. What you want to do is just cut out the middle of a big monster and prune every few years."

I smiled. In our absence from one another I'd forgotten his woodman's lore, his enthusiasm, the pleasure he took in his work, and the pleasure I took in hearing about it.

"I'm babbling."

"You know I love anything to do with trees."

He pushed hair off my forehead. "You have brown flecks in one of your irises."

I smiled again. Scarcely a foot from the end of the platform bed—no headboard, no dust ruffle—stood his dresser. Its surface was cluttered with universally male belongings—slips of paper, coins, a belt buckle, cardboard coasters from bars, a brass letter holder whose slots were empty. Beside a ceramic ginger jar lamp with a flecked paper shade lay a thin leather wallet whose tender upward curve, shaped by day after day in a rear pocket, pierced me. Beneath the sheet, I fit my palm to the roundness of his butt and felt goose bumps rise on the baby-soft skin.

"What are you looking at?"

"Your room. I've imagined what it might look like. Being in here is like . . . When I was young and visited a friend I was always afraid of their parents' bedrooms. They seemed sanctuaries, somehow, not so much private as simply—no trespassing, off-limits. I'd go to the other end of the house to answer the phone rather than step over the threshold of another mother's room." I sat up and pulled the sheet over my breasts. "Now I'm the one who's babbling."

"I like to hear you babble. You don't babble enough." Unembarrassed, he sprawled naked beside me. "You're still watching. What are you looking at now?"

"The ceiling. Whit stuck fluorescent stars and moons all over his ceiling, but I took them down."

"When?"

"A while ago. After the snow." That sleepless night of the erotic dream. Here was a fantasy fulfilled, his arms bunched around a pillow, his legs covered in dark hair, languorously crossed at the ankles.

"Why did you?"

I ran my finger over the sheet's raveling edge and turned away from the ceiling to face him. Over his shoulder I glimpsed a clock on the bedside table. We'd spent barely twenty-five minutes in our loving. Whit's private sky lasted twenty-two. "It was time."

He leaned and kissed behind my ear. "Old Spice," I said. "You're wearing Old Spice. I haven't smelled Old Spice since—" Since I couldn't remember and didn't want to. "Remember when you buzz-cut the pampas grass that first time we met? I was raking leaves and I was so sad, and you made me talk to you." I remembered the grief, the heavy-lidded, thick-handed, swollen-limbed inertia, so different from this limp, spent inertia of release. Release from ecstasy. I laughed aloud at the thought. "And you made me laugh. You said, 'Look, she has teeth.'" My fingers found a hard bump at his crown, a rounded knob. "What's this?"

"A wen."

"Aren't they supposed to be lucky?"

"Whatever you say, ma'am." He pulled my hand down and wedged his chin in my neck. "Why did you come, Laura?"

Lora, he said, soft as smoke. "I needed . . . forgiveness. And . . . comfort. Consolation."

"Because of Whit," he said. "Because you'd been thinking about him?"

No, I thought, but didn't say. Why tell Elliot all I'd discovered about Russ, and Darrell, and the bastardized stucco mansion on the corner? There had been enough revelations and ample heartbreak for one day. And they were my troubles, not Elliot's. I came because I'd felt betrayed and abandoned, and I seized on him for sympathy, for tenderness. "I wanted to . . . talk. To apologize and be friends again. I didn't plan to, I didn't think we'd—"

"I know." He lifted my hand and turned my wedding band around and around on my finger. "I have a friend whose wedding ring is tattooed on his finger because he's a rock climber and can't wear a real one."

"Tattooed wedding rings. God. I feel like Mrs. Robinson."

"Who's that?" he grinned, and moved over me. "Dick and Jane's mother?"

Only when you're home, standing on still-shaking legs in the shower while the warm water sheets over you do you finally think instead of feel. Only then do you think about the recklessness, and the risk, and that he's closer to your son's age than yours. *I've betrayed Russ*, you think. Is it different from how he has betrayed me? *I've committed adultery*, you think, that ponderous, legalistic phrase, *But I didn't mean to. It was an accident.*

Even as he grows stiff and thick against your belly you say, "I can't." Because he must know—he must— that this can't happen again. "Elliot—"

"Once more," he says, misunderstanding, and knees apart your legs and slips his hands beneath the small of your back and arches you against him and buries himself in you again. "Just once more."

Chapter Sixteen

IT HAD A TECHNICAL, SCIENTIFIC NAME: DOWNBURST. BUT no amount of prediction or preparation would have changed the outcome or the effects.

It was the utter unexpectedness that was so shocking: at nine in the morning; in April. Barely a day after Elliot. Daylight Saving Time's morning chill had lifted and it was open-window time again, the sweet two-month period—three if June cooperated—when the air is balmy and caressing and birdsong is loud enough to distract. Where had the feather-light birds taken shelter, I wondered afterward.

In two minutes the entire pale morning sky curdled and churned and blackened as though an evil spell had overtaken it. I raced to slam down windows where loose papers had been oddly sucked to the screens as though vacuumed, then stood watching the silvery undersides of leaves flattening in unison, a telltale storm herald I've always loved. But when the massive trunks heaved and pitched, when the wind roared as though I was standing beside an interstate highway, I retreated to stand in a door frame, feeling foolish.

Eight minutes, start to finish.

Later, dozens and dozens of what-I-was-doing tales emerged. A ream of inkjet paper beneath his arm, Tom Stukes watched five car windshields in an Office Depot parking lot burst from the drop in air pressure. Gayle Lowry was making her bed when she saw the three-story oak outside her bedroom window lean ominously. She made it outdoors just in time to watch it crash through the wing where she'd been stooping seconds earlier. She'd stood on the sidewalk in the brief lashing rain and sobbed.

Miraculously, not a single life was lost in a freak weather event dryly defined as a strong downdraft with an outrush of damaging winds on or near the ground. But its severity left us declared a disaster area.

"It's hard to say who was out first," Russ said that night, "the insurance reps or the rubberneckers." I was one of the latter.

A cautious Munchkin venturing out after the Wicked Witch's departure, I opened the front door to an unearthly quiet. The scene was breathtaking, both fascinating and disturbing: a raw, theatrical, savage beauty. In eight minutes the streetscape was transformed from twentieth-century neighborhood into a prehistoric tableau, as though roaming dinosaurs had carelessly ravaged it. Electrical wires and telephone cables snaked menacingly across streets and driveways. They were limp swaybacked jump ropes between the schoolgirl hands of listing poles. Some lines were pulled tautly down at forty-five-degree angles, held captive beneath fallen trees as though a giant thumb pinned them, and I thought ludicrously of the finger game I'd played with my children. *One two three four, I declare thumb war.* As though hurled by the gods, a limb as tall as I was driven bolt upright into our yard, looking for all the world like a newly planted sapling. It took both hands to pull it out, and a hole five inches deep was left behind when I finally succeeded.

Stoops and sills and roofs were plastered with wet blown leaves; fences and swing sets and patio furniture dangled branches, accidental decorations. A construction site Port-O-Let, its bright blue hue intrusive in the green eye-level world, lay crushed like a shoebox. In a just world, such destruction would be reserved for the naked bleakness of winter, not the full-foliage lushness of spring, when forsythia and deutzia and spirea, those lovely Latinate names, bloomed; not when lawns were verdant and thick and striped with recent mowing; not when red coral bells and blue forget-me-nots and white candytuft—

though wet and windblown—blossomed gaily and obliviously beneath windblown detritus.

But the trees. My God, the trees.

Forty and fifty feet tall, they lay across streets like pick-up sticks; gargantuan, decades-old denizens felled in seconds. They stretched from yard to yard, not the vulnerable pines, gangly and top-heavy culprits routinely blamed for their tendency to topple. But the stately, better-loved, more-preferred poplars and oaks and maples. My pin oak was spared but I grieved for the others, helpless woody giants now horizontal and humbled. Their massive immensity was revealed in entirety to us mortals now, but their nobility had been cruelly robbed. And at least they were slain whole. Smaller species were quartered and halved with gashes, their pale tender gullets exposed like sore throats. The most humiliated specimens were the ones that had been sheared off in some random reasonless selection. Branchless, leafless, standing alone in a yard or park, they looked like Popsicle sticks a child holds in a fist and snaps in half with a single press of his thumb. Splintered, jagged, like a bone poking through flesh. How can something be called a stump when it's still fifteen feet high?

Within the hour people stirred in houses darkened and silenced without electricity or telephones, and cleanup began. Hadn't Russ told me this? We're human beings. Human beings adjust and

pick themselves up and begin again. They *resume.*
Power crews shut down live, lethal wires. Parents
retrieved children from schools where they'd
crouched in storage rooms and auditoriums. Sirens
wailed without ceasing; policemen gestured and
whistled at busy intersections presided over by
defunct and dangling stoplights. City road crews
established priorities and went to work to liberate
the most impassable, most frequently used, most necessary streets. Telephone companies did the same,
gauging damage and repairing business service first.

Lack of electricity and telephones stymied com-
merce, but residential neighborhoods had suffered
most. Few office parks or downtown multistoried
buildings or shopping malls are built under towering
trees, after all. Their plantings are done after construction, and, as Elliot predicted, the wind ripped
the guts from those Bradford pears, their perfect
heart shapes sliced down the middle.

As though Greensboro were a medieval city cut
off by plague, utility crews were contracted from other
cities and regions. Regular workdays were sacrificed
to need, so that we grew accustomed to the flashing
lights of repair trucks at all hours of the day or night.
People joked about living in Tornado Alley and being
"telephonically challenged." They fired up gas grills,
and thanked God for cell phone car chargers, and
read magazines in strip mall Laundromats. They

pressed coolers into refrigerator service and bought bagged ice. They went to bed at eight because there was nothing else to do.

"This is how it was for Laura Ingalls Wilder," I told Ebie when she complained.

"It must have been really boring to live back then," she replied. "I wish I hadn't burned my rainbow candle. Now I need it."

I stifled a sudden image of Jenny and her fancy candles. Had they still been scattered on Elliot's tables the afternoon we—and stifled that thought as well, certain that the memory alone would pink my face, heat it like a fever with the thought of that pure, sweet release—

I couldn't go there. Not mentally, not literally. For two weeks I never saw him. He left at first light and returned after dark. Every tree service for five surrounding counties had more work than they could handle. As with electricity and telephone line repairmen, tree crews had priorities too. Homeowners with trees literally through the roof were referred to the city because exposure meant compulsory condemnation. Otherwise, first priority went to homeowners with trees lying on roofs that were intact. Next on the list were previous clients clamoring for assistance, and eventually, as Elliot told Ebie, "the rest."

So, my mind churning with remorse, memory,

and waiting for the other shoe to drop, I walked. Walked Liberty Ave and beyond, or drove familiar streets whose shade I'd taken for granted, now startlingly sunlit. It wasn't simply the leaflessness but the absence of the trees themselves. Wings of houses and backyards once hidden were now revealed. Crinkled tarps appeared on rooftops as temporary protection from the elements. One morning I drove past a bungalow whose entire front facade had been ripped away by a falling tree, leaving the rooms as open as a dollhouse. An upstairs bedroom wallpapered in yellow sprigged with pink flowers was exposed for all the world to view, and I was sad for the awful unprivacy of it.

Once I parked and got out and stood at the base of a fallen giant. I gazed at a horizontal eight-foot disc of grass clipped as a putting green, where purple violets still bloomed perkily, if crazily sideways. Behind it, in stark contrast, was a craggy crude circle of protruding roots and chunked clay and beneath that was a gaping maw of raw, red hole. The long trunk itself lay three feet above the ground, supported not only by the width of its spreading roots, but by splayed branches that had broken its fall. I hoisted myself upon the trunk and stood on a bark path leading to branches radiating outward like spokes on a wheel. Their leaves were still lush and full; they hadn't yet received the message that their days were numbered, their source of sustenance severed. The tree had fallen across a backyard, and beneath its staggering weight was a plastic playhouse crushed like a paper cup. The slain woody mammoth had landed squarely on a single-car garage, inverting its pointed shingled roof. Inside, tools still hung in neat configuration on a pegboard.

I was standing on a child's dream come true, a windfall gift. The trunk was too wide to fall from, easily imagined as a natural bridge across a make-believe ravine where a make-believe waterfall thundered into a river foaming with make-believe piranhas. Or no, instead, the trunk was a horse's girth to be straddled, a mountaintop to be scaled, a pirate's plank to be walked. It even offered a choice when the branches parted—which road to take? Within the brushy thicket of leaves and branches lay the stuff of fairytale: an enchanted forest complete with princesses, panthers, dragons. Here was the best kind of childhood hiding place because it was accessible and known and safe. "It's just *leaves*," I could nearly hear a small boy scoff at a timid playmate from the tangle of spiky branches, "no briars. Let's play army. See? I'm camouflaged."

But I was a grown-up, and I stood on the trunk and studied the treetop, surprised and melancholy at how naked the behemoth looked in repose, all that foliage no more than a lacy nightcap. I couldn't help viewing the skewed branches as limbs on a corpse, stiff and akimbo with rigor mortis.

"Fallen trees look like broccoli stalks," Ebie had said. "Bett says they look like—" she giggled, testing my tolerance, "—like penises." I hadn't scolded her; the phallic description was too apt.

And in another arena, too appropriate. Elliot.

"It was like a dream," Whit had said after his near miss with a car. That was an apt description, too, of an intimacy no one had planned or intended or anticipated. Like a dream.

Then one Sunday afternoon I finally saw him outside. He looked up from cleaning tools, saw me on the other side of the fence, and made the smallest gesture of a wave. "Laura."

I felt rooted, shy, embarrassed, mute. Six months ago we'd stood in these same places as strangers. Two weeks ago we'd been lovers. What were we now?

"I've been busy," he said.

I smiled at the absurdity of the understatement.

"Overwhelmed is closer to it, I guess."

"You look exhausted."

"I am," he admitted. "Are you good?"

Good? That was absurd too, wasn't it? How, good? Feeling good? A good girl? Neither of those. "Yes," I said. "I'm good. It's whatever-the-market-will-bear time, isn't it?"

"It's not the money, it's . . ."

"Admit it. You're reveling in it."

His grin was sheepish, and I was reminded again of the boy he was. "Because it's my kind of tree work. I don't kill anything, just helping people, saving the trees I can." He looked up into the pin oak. "You were lucky."

"'Lucky'?"

"Your oak survived."

Lucky, yet again. I walked toward it, leaned against the scaly bark and ran my finger down a lighter trail where ivy had once climbed up it. "I feel differently about trees now."

"Different how?"

I sighed. Because the same tall trees I loved had wreaked the worst damage. Those splendid giants had shuddered and toppled and taken smaller brothers down with them or split others down the middle with their bulk; it was those towering trees that crashed onto houses and streets and cars, upending sidewalks as easily as if their concrete squares were playing cards. Trees had once been noble, benevolent giants to me. But I'd discovered that my mourning was misplaced, my affection unrequited. "I don't think I can explain it."

Elliot stood and wiped his hands on his jeans and walked to the fence. "Try."

How could I describe my new ambivalence? I tried. "Trees had an animate life to me before the storm. They waved and shed and grew. They whispered and shaded and turned colors and shook their heads. They were friendly and giving and I was their advocate."

Elliot leaned his head, waiting, and ran two fingers down the jaw I'd run my fingers down. I swallowed and looked away.

"And now?" he pressed, bringing me back.

I thought of the terror and the damage, the families displaced from uninhabitable homes, the extensive ruin. "And now trees are only overgrown plants to me, plants that can just as easily smash a house as shed leaves. Trees don't *care* if I'm on their side, they don't care. They grow and shade and shelter but they kill and destroy, too. They'd fall on me and those I love in a single second. Trees can't help you or can't save you. Sometimes they're victims, sometimes they're villains. In either case they're indifferent giants, neither good nor bad. They're just . . . things."

"Laura," he said, pained.

"It's not a bad feeling; it's just an altered feeling." I changed the subject. "When the Duke Power man finally showed up to work on our transformer I was so happy to see him that I took our just-delivered take-out pizza to him. He sat in his truck and ate it."

"That's where I've been doing most of my eating. Sleeping, too."

"Eat more." He was wiry, sinewy from too much

work and too little food. "You're too thin." I spoke
without thinking how I sounded: like a mother.

Someone knocked on a window pane. I turned.
It was Russ, pointing to his watch. His construction
sites bore few effects of the storm. After all, they were
already ravaged.

I waved and nodded. I hadn't confronted Russ
with Anne's revelations about his involvement down
the street, or his giving Darrell no choice but to leave
Lucas Con. A conversation about either would
expose the other. As pathetic a confession as it is, lack
of electricity requires all your attention and survival
skills. Maybe that's how Ma and Pa Ingalls managed
their marriage, I thought. Russ and I had moved
along in the literal and physical dark, reading by candlelight, going to bed early, and yes, having sex.

Elliot was watching me, and I felt flayed and raw,
unsure whether what nagged and pursued me was
temporary love or carnal lust or a naive crush or my
dead son Whit or my living husband Russ or
whether to laugh or cry or jump over the fence and
beg Elliot Hatcher to take me on a tree job with
him, in the police car with him, away, anywhere. Just
with him.

The tapping sounded again but I didn't turn
around and acknowledge it. "I have to take Ebie to
her youth group at church."

Elliot bowed his head, and I faced the black

ringlets. What he said was so soft that it wasn't even a question. "Are you sorry."

Friendship can become attraction, but they're not interchangeable. With one, there's no going back. Sorry? "Look at me, Elliot."

And he did, with eyes so black they seemed all pupil. "No," I told him. "I'm not sorry."

Chapter Seventeen

"HARK, THE HERALD ANGELS SHOUT," EBIE SANG BESIDE ME in the front seat, "one more week 'til I get out!"

She was crowing about her cast coming off, but the lyrics were Windsor's version of the traditional Christmas carol. *Grab your ball and grab your chain, run like hell for the nearest train. No more books and no more thinking, back to the life of sex and drinking. Hark, the herald angels shout—*

She drew a smiley face on the window pane yellowed with May pollen. "You don't take walks with Anne anymore. Aren't you friends still?"

I shifted the dashboard vent's direction. Clearly, I'd been trading on Ebie's obliviousness and the self-absorption of childhood too long. Experts advise that when a child asks about sex to answer no more than necessary. "Friends fade in and out like a voice in a wind. Sometimes they're stronger and sometimes they're weaker," I replied. "Like you and Bett last winter, when she was spending so much time with her band, remember?" I'd hidden from Anne once in the grocery store, turned down the bread aisle and hurried toward produce, thanking God for the supermarket's immenseness I'd often cursed. After that, I changed grocery stores.

"When you're not *not* friends," I said now to Ebie, "but you're not quite friends, either. Do you know what I mean?"

"Like what happened with you and Elliot after my arm got broken."

Did this come under "asking more" or was it just my heightened awareness, the state of suspension I uneasily inhabited? "I think Anne has gone to Rollins this week to help Adele move out of her dorm."

Ebie hummed, and I couldn't help but mentally supply the lyrics. *Back to the life of sex and drinking.* Not for the first time, I wondered if Whit had had sex. He was nineteen when he died. Surely he had, surely. I wanted him to have had that sweet experience. Maybe he'd made love with Adele, who'd have done anything for him the way I once would have for Russ. "When you have sex with someone," I'd told him hesitantly before he went to boarding school, "you forever own a piece of them and they forever own a piece of you."

"Mom." He'd objected to the personal topic.

"*And* this is a very small state and you're going to run into her for the next fifty years." I punted with levity, knowing he'd heard the more important advice.

And now I owned a piece of Elliot Hatcher, and he me. The thought of our sex made my hands limp on the steering wheel. "Besides, it's still hard to take a walk," I added to Ebie, and pointed to an angular heap of jagged branches obstructing a sidewalk.

This, at least, was truthful. More than three weeks after the storm's slaughter, life had returned to normal in most venues. Greensboro had progressed from horror to wonder to sorrow, and on to daily tolerance.

Electricity and telephones were restored, city services were back on schedule, and housing repairs were under way. Cleanup had begun in earnest in neighborhoods, and never had the wallets of wealthier homeowners been more apparent; yard services moved with astonishing swiftness to hand-pick leaves and branches from lawns and haul them away in slat-sided trucks. But for the greater majority of us, the debris had to be deposited somewhere, and curbs were clogged with leaf piles lacking any of autumn's glorious hues. Instead of fall's crisp reds and yellows and oranges, these leaves on collected branches had shriveled into dull browns and ashy blacks, stark and withered compared to the surrounding lushness of May.

"Number two pile," Ebie said.

We'd assigned numbers to the debris to entertain ourselves during errands. "Number ones" were "anywhere but here" branches pulled from yards by weary and impatient homeowners who knew nothing else to do with them but drag them to the curb and wait for the limbs to be picked up by already overextended collection trucks. "Two" were the neat sticks of one length sawed and bundled by those folks who helplessly follow collection regulations even in times of disaster, a moot lawfulness since the city had dropped length requirements for the foreseeable future. Governing rules had fallen by the wayside simply to make streets two-laned and passable.

"Trunk chunks," Ebie said. "Number three." These were heavy sections of chainsawed logs propped on curbsides like seats at summer camp or an illustration from Paul Bunyan. They were clunky nuisances bearing proverbial rings of age, some with darker cores like candy nougat fillings or pencil lead.

"That one looks like Elliot's table," Ebie said.

The black oak. "When did you see Elliot's table?"

"Mom. The snow party."

Oh. Yes.

"They're naked," Ebie said of the sparser "Number Four" piles: stiff tuberous roots looking like carrots or hardened arteries.

"Since when do you say nay-kid instead of nekkid?"

"That's how Bett says it."

Reason enough at eleven years old. Finally came Number Fives, the pale cones of sawdust that would become a fresh cushion on a school or park playground. Ebie shut the car door. "Spirit Week starts on Monday."

"What's that?"

"Mom, you *know*," she said, "when we get to dress up different every day at school. Pajama Day, Team Day, Patriotic Day, Tacky Day." She ticked off the categories and sighed. "Bett will win Tacky Day. She bought a tiger-print skirt and one-shouldered purple turtleneck at the mall. I need a garbageless lunch tomorrow to be kind to the environment or else I don't get to par-ti-ci-pate in Spirit Week,"she carefully enunciated in her best principal's voice.

I laughed at the irony. A garbageless lunch, with so much trash on our streets.

A utility truck bearing a load of skeletal branches lumbered up the street, its gears clanking like old radiators. It hissed, grinding to a halt before a Number Four pile. "Fart truck," Ebie said with elaborate weariness, and kicked at a branch. "I'm ready for this stuff to be gone."

I was sick of it, too. Sick of the ceaseless clack and clatter of chippers and shredders and stump grinders.

Sick of the drilled, high-pitched whine of chain saws, and the thin, repetitive *pingpingping* warnings of reversing trucks. Sick of orange cones and orange vests and orange helmets and orange Asplundh trucks. And sick with a few private categories: guilt, desire, deception, fear, lust, anticipation. Sick with the strain of uncertainty: what to do next and whether I wanted to. Whether he did. I vacillated between feeling ridiculous and repulsive, and wanting more. "Sex is like money or garage space," I'd laughed with Anne once, "you use all you have and want more."

"Is that a collective you?" Anne laughed back.

It was inconceivable that what had happened between us didn't show on my face. Every action or gesture or comment felt freighted with waiting. I wondered if Darrell was as brightly animated and talkative with Anne as I was with Russ, dredging up small details to fill conversation gaps that on any other morning or evening would be no more than comfortable silences. "You look nice, haven't seen that shirt in a while,"; "The car's getting better gas mileage since the tune-up."

Or was it less animation than agitation? Were my overly-careful exchanges a determined pretense to appear natural, normal? I was jangled and nervous that any compliment or comment or ordinary domestic task was a signal of atonement or admission.

"Thanks for washing my brush," Russ said, or "Don't take out the trash, that's Ebie's chore."

"It's not Tuesday," Ebie said. "You only do laundry on Tuesdays."

"And when did you begin ironing?" Russ asked. He examined the sleeves, puckered at the cuff seam. "Just go ahead and take my shirts to the cleaners, would you?"

But then Darrell's affair was ongoing, and mine had been a single straying. Far less adulterous, wasn't it? Unplanned, accidental, motivated by a longing for comfort and consolation, not sex, not love. Or was it no more than a besotted, passionate impulse? I hadn't seduced Elliot, had I? Hadn't he wanted me as well? We'd been mutually consenting adults, hadn't we?

As if, the retort goes. As if a morality chart—good, bad, worse—exists for extramarital sex. I didn't want to know the answers to those questions. Living with the tension of infidelity, straddling deceit and desire, was difficult enough. Not that I could seek answers—or reassurance, or relief—from Elliot. His crew was still busy, and had moved to the jobs beyond any neighborhood where I could drive by and glimpse him working.

"Out in the boonies," Ebie reported. For she sought him out the few hours he was home in the evenings, and, too hungry for scraps of information buried in her chatter, I didn't tell her to leave him in peace.

In the mornings I'd brush my teeth and through our open bathroom window upstairs occasionally hear dishes clink in Elliot's kitchen below. I glimpsed shadowy movements in his bed-room—a bedroom I now knew—no differently than I'd glimpsed Meany Matheny, and think I was going mad. It couldn't go on.

Until finally, it didn't. One Thursday afternoon the telephone rang, and a shoe dropped.

"Laura." *Lora.*

"Elliot, what—"

"Please come. Please." *Just once more.*

Chapter Eighteen

HE WAS STANDING INSIDE, WAITING.

If only I had asked *Why are you home this hour of the day?*

But the haircut stopped me. The lovely boyish tangle of ebony curls was gone, shaved away to shadow just as Whit had done to himself two springs ago in support of Chris Goss. Chris Goss, the classmate stricken with cancer who had died, like Whit. And like Whit, Elliot looked young and vulnerable, a bald baby bird lacking feathery down. "Oh, Elliot." I'd come so far from grief, but fought welling tears and an urge to reach and touch the stiff velvety prickles of sprouting hair. "What have you done?"

He grabbed my elbow, nearly dragging me to the bedroom, and began lifting my T-shirt before I could even raise my arms. "Elliot, wait—"

But he sat on the bed, yanked the zipper to my shorts, fumbled with my bra, pressed his face to my bound breasts. "Do it, God," he urged fiercely, but before I'd found the bra's clasp, he pulled me bodily onto the mattress.

Rising on his knees he stripped his shirt off without unbuttoning it and, flinging it down, pinned me beneath him and roughly kneed apart my legs. Denim chafed my thighs and metal rivets gouged my belly. I reached for the waistband of his jeans but he impatiently shoved my arms away and jerked the pants down only low enough to free his penis. He was frantic, a starving man.

"Elliot—" I tried to hold him close, but he wasn't interested in tenderness, or sensuality. I reached for a pillow, but he grasped both my wrists with one hand above my head, grabbed my hair in his other fist so that my head, my eyes, were angled away from him. The buttons of his shirt wadded beneath my face pressed painfully into my cheek. "Wait—"

But instead he grunted, ramming into me so deeply that I jerked in pain and gasped beneath him. His body was all sharp elbows and knees, and his tight belly slapped against mine with the leatherlike noise of skin on skin. I felt impaled, gutted. He released my hair and held on to my hipbone instead, as though for leverage, to spike further into me. Gripped too tightly in his other hands to lower them, my knuckles scraped the wall with his thrusts. "Elliot!" I cried, panicked.

This was slaking, not sex; a clawed, bestial coupling unrelated to loving. I wasn't Laura beneath him. I was nothing but an available cavity to receive his bucking. "Stop!" Suddenly more furious than frightened, I twisted and heaved. "Get off me!"

Suddenly, it was over. The terror in my cries reached him, or perhaps he was only spent and finished with me. I turned on my side, curled, and cried with confusion and pain as I hadn't since Whit's death. I'd been razed and raped no differently than the house on the corner, the felled trees.

The mattress moved, and I felt his knees at my back. "I'm sorry, Laura, I'm sorry," he bleated. "Look at me, please look at me." He leaned over me, pleated the sheet in his fingers and wiped tears from my face. "I didn't mean to, I'm sorry, I'm sorry, it was an accident."

I shrugged away his touch with my shoulder, angry now rather than bewildered. Everything hurt or ached or stung. Crotch tendons he'd spread too widely, my breasts chapped from the bra he hadn't even let me remove. "Rough sex is not an accident." My genitals throbbed. "You *hurt* me."

He shook his head and tried to thread his fingers through mine. "I don't know why. I needed to just . . . feel something."

I jerked my hand away from his and sat up. "'Something'?"

"Something, no—someone alive."

I stared at him, disgusted. "It could have been anyone, then."

"What?"

"Under you. For you to—" I choked on the word, "—plug."

"No." A range of unreadable emotions played over his face. "Yes. I . . ."

I got out of bed and pulled on my T-shirt and shorts, stuffing my underwear into a pocket. I walked to the window and parted the blinds with my fingers. I don't know what I was looking for; Ebie was babysitting, Russ was at work. Perhaps I was simply letting the anger subside, hoping it would.

There was the leyland cypress I'd planted to shield Mrs. Matheny's ugly house from ours. They're fast growers, leyland cypresses, and so it had. The tree was only a foot tall at planting, and I'd anchored it to the ground with wire, threading the wire through a length of rubber hosing where it touched the trunk so the metal couldn't cut the bark. Couldn't chafe and scrape in storms and wind and open the bark, exposing the sapling to disease and pests.

But sometime while I wasn't watching the tether wire had snapped. Yet the tree had gone on growing, its trunk seamlessly swallowing a section of hose. The two ends protruded from the trunk like a tube accidentally left in a body during surgery. I could blow into it and feel my breath come out the other side. The hose had become part of the tree itself, but removing the hose now would kill the tree. It had healed over and around the inorganic object and had thrived despite it. Not so differently from human beings who heal around the scar tissue of deep hurt. Human beings like me. Regret and shame and anger fused: I would grow around Elliot Hatcher, too.

"Laura," Elliot said in a muffled voice.

I turned and looked at him. His knees were raised and his arms rested on them, and his face was bowed and hidden between them. "You've made it easy for me, Elliot. Easy to end this—whatever we're doing." I sucked on my bleeding knuckles, then thrust them toward him in a fist. "Look at this. What would you like me to tell Russ about these? That the boy next door manhandled me during sex, drove his dick into me and bound my hands, and the whole time had his clothes on?"

"Please come over here, please just . . . touch me."

"*Touch* you? The way you just *touched* me?" With his posture of suffering and pale outline of his shaved head, Elliot's youth struck me all over again. He was a boy, and I was a fool. "That was rape, Elliot. *Rape.* Are you that young, that stupid, to believe the nonsense that women *want* it like that? That we fantasize about being raped, like the skin mags declare?"

"Laura." He was crying now, reaching blindly for me without lifting his head.

But I was blind, too, with disbelief and fury. "No, Elliot. I welcomed you to my home and my life, and I defended you to my husband and my friends, and what do you do for me? Betray me. You let my child be injured. And now you injure me. My feelings, my body. You find someone else to hurt. Because you won't find me anymore." Face to the wall, he didn't answer, and I left him there, striding to the door on jellied legs and slammed it behind me.

And when, only a few hours later, the other shoe dropped, it was ugly. Fierce and roiling black as a thundercloud.

Russ shoved the bank papers in his briefcase. "It's only an appraisal!"

"You had no intention of getting a second mortgage," I shot back. "We don't *need* a second mortgage."

"Well, why not have some cash to do a few projects? You could uplight your precious trees, or hire a lawn service, or put in the rose garden you've talked about, or an outside hearth on the terrace. They're all the rage. I'm putting one in at—" he stopped himself, but I knew what he meant to say: the new house down the street. His stealth project.

"I don't want a lawn service or a rose garden *or* an outside hearth."

"Sure, why bother? You can go over and hang around Elliot Hatcher's grill. Maybe he'll take *you* skitching. Maybe he'll nearly kill *you*."

I ignored the retort. "Since your business is expanding so exponentially, maybe you'd like to turn Whit's room into an office."

"Better an office than a shrine," Russ said dramatically.

"Have you noticed his room is cleared? Do you ever even walk in it?"

He pressed his lips together, inhaled deeply, and reversed to the argument's starting point. "I was only seeing what our house would hypothetically sell for. It's *only* a price, *only* an estimate."

"Why should I believe you, Russ? You said Darrell *only* wanted to do kitchens and baths for the rest of his life."

His eyes flashed.

"I know it all, Russ. You fired Darrell because he wouldn't play by your rules. You fired him because he wouldn't agree to razing and rebuilding and destroying all the charm of Liberty Ave. So you can build houses that look like that, that Magic Kingdom castle down there. Don't deny it, Russ. I *know.* Anne told me."

He looked up at the ceiling as though imploring patience. "Of course she did. Mouth of the South. She tells you about her *sex* life. Do you tell her about ours?"

I glared at him, refusing to be roped and trapped into that. To choke on my own hypocrisy. "There's not one thing Darrell did wrong."

"Oh, except for screwing around on his wife. Did you tell Anne that?"

"And did you ever ask Darrell if he actually was, or was just a victim of gossip, office gossip at that?"

"I'm not his father. I have more dignity than that."

"Dignity? Do you know what being fired does to dignity? To be fired by a *friend*?"

"Did you make me a monster?"

"What are you talking about?"

"When you had your, your *chat* with Anne."

"She didn't even come to talk about Darrell. She came to—" I stopped myself.

"Ye-es?" Contempt edged his drawl. "Have you framed the newspaper photo? If you need another someone tacked one on the office bulletin board. So I get to pass it a dozen times every day."

"I haven't seen Anne at all since the day she came by. It's over for us as friends, Russ. Can't you see? It's not just your relationship with Darrell that's finished, it's mine with Anne."

"Like you've been spending any time with her in the past few months." The sarcasm was thick. He wadded a paper towel and lobbed it toward the trash can where, for the thousandth time in our marriage, it fell instead on the floor. "Hell, why *not* sell our house? Someone almost broke in, not that it seemed to worry you overly much. Mind on other things, et cetera."

"Don't throw that at me. It's not like you're ever here."

"This is going around in circles. I'm not selling the house. I simply wanted to see whether its value has changed along with Liberty Ave's. Thanks to all the goddamn trees, the street's value has dropped since the storm. And thanks to a couple of transient renters. Christ, it's May, and those fake Christmas icicles are still hanging from the gutters four doors down. When Meany Matheny's house goes on the market—and it *will*—I'm buying it."

"So you can tear it down too?"

"You've complained for years about the way it looks. Go ahead, deny *that*."

I stretched my arms to the table and leaned my weight on them, exhausted with arguing. There was nothing to win, and it came down to a single issue. "I don't trust you anymore, Russ. You haven't been honest about Darrell, and you weren't honest about having our house appraised, and you weren't honest about your involvement with that monstrosity down the street."

"But *you*, of course, are honest as the day is long." He rose from the table and elaborately retied the belt of his robe and walked toward the stairs and the shadow that had lengthened and shortened between us finally thickened into something solid and immoveable. Hand on the newel post, my husband paused, and turned, and stared at me. "The feeling's mutual, Laura. Goodnight."

The fight had left me panting; racing, shallow breaths. There were no sleeping pills in a pouch, nothing to blot out what had happened between us in the last minutes and the last months. There were no chores to occupy me, petty tasks of avoidance and denial. Bills were paid, dishes were washed, plants were watered. I switched on the television and flicked through channels. For a month the local news shows had run variations of the same stories: human interest tales of repairs and rebuilding, neighborhood hero anecdotes interspersed with the most recent damage statistics and cleanup efforts by our tireless civil servants.

I expected familiar footage. All fallen trees are eventually reduced to sticks and leaves and sawdust, and all talking heads sound the same. "Seen it," Whit would say, and I'd seen this closeup, too, the side view of a mammoth root ball as tall as a six-foot man, the attached hunk of clay and roots the size of a small car. Roots stuck out like witchy hair from soil that held a geology lesson. Eight inches of clay, then sedimentary, then—what was the next layer called?

"...typical size," the reporter droned. "The cavity left behind is easily ten feet across and four feet deep."

I stood and drew the shutters, and prepared for a sleepless night. In Whit's room.

"Until today's tragic accident," the reporter said, "not a single life was lost on account of the April storm."

I turned and peered at the screen. Yellow caution tape clumsily circled a wooded lot and flashing lights circled noiselessly from a police car parked beside a mammoth sawed-off tree trunk standing nearly bolt upright. The reporter stuck a microphone into someone's face. "What would you estimate the trunk and root ball weighed?"

The man turned on his heels without answering. I knew that face from a glorious October day: Diego's.

The rejected reporter solemnly faced the camera again though the film had obviously been taped earlier, in daytime. "Apparently, Steve, the child was playing army in the hole left by the upended root ball."

I squinted, trying to discern the figures huddled at the side of the screen. The clearing looked familiar too, and wasn't that truck—

"You can imagine how inviting that cavern looked to a boy of six," the journalist said solemnly to the desk anchor.

Oh, I could imagine very well. Princesses and dragons and jungles full of pretend-army men. A cave in the ground provided just for you, with craggy walls you could climb or bore sticks into digging for buried treasure; dangling roots you could yank as if they were Tarzan's vine swing, and so many places to hide, to squat and carefully arrange toy soldiers while the big boys with saws worked above you, making it too noisy to even talk. You could talk and call and yell commands like a sergeant in your pretend play and no one would make fun of you. No one would even hear little Theodore Allen Strickland the third, as he'd so self-importantly informed and charmed me. Teddy. Tow-headed Teddy Strickland whose smiling photograph filled the screen.

As the tape rolled again, one of the workers dropped to the ground, face buried in his hands. Someone who was thin. Someone with scarcely any hair. Someone who was Elliot. *I do the ground work* he'd assured me long ago.

"This tree's trunk is over eight feet in diameter, an unimaginable weight," the reporter kept on. He kept on and on, relentless. But I knew, I already knew. "When Elliot Hatcher, the workman on the

SUSAN KELLY

job, sawed through it, the root ball rocked back with its own tonnage and pulled the trunk back over, dropping into its original position."

It had closed like a jaw over an unseen crouching child playing army in the magical private cavern.

This was why Elliot had been home in the middle of the day. This was why he'd raped me. Why he wanted to *feel something*. Why his head had been bowed. Not with apology to me, but with misery and responsibility and terrible, terrible grief. *You have no idea what it feels like to lose someone,* I'd spat in that sterile hospital corridor.

Elliot. Oh, Elliot. My sweet sorrowing guilt-stricken boy.

I didn't mean to, it was an accident, I'm sorry, Laura, I'm sorry. Forgive me.

He'd needed someone to hold him and stroke him and reassure him that it wasn't his fault, that what had happened was a terrible, terrible accident. I'd needed a son and a lover and he'd been both to me. He'd needed a mother and a lover, and I'd only been one for him.

"The Strickland family will file no charges since the incident was clearly a tragic accident," the reporter said gravely. "Back to you, Steve."

I thought of the blond man who'd held Teddy's hand, his father. An accident. "But that's not fair," I'd objected to Whit's driver's ed scenario. Laughing,

276

Whit had asked back, "If a deer jumps into the road and crashes into your car, do you sue the deer?"

"Tomorrow should be balmy and clear," the weatherman was saying, "no sign of wind *or* drought." He smiled, pleased with his optimistic news.

I switched off the set, hurried to the window, and peered round the cypress tree, straining to see through the slats of the cheap stockade fence. The house next door was dark. I walked to the living room, climbed onto the sofa, and looked harder, closer. Tonight the street light wasn't shining; the light bothered Elliot as much as it bothered me. Thank God he's asleep, I thought. I could be up and over there tomorrow before he left for work to comfort and console him the way he'd done for me. *It dogs you and drags you and takes a long time I'd say, but you'll come out of it, Elliot, you will. As I did. Because of you.*

A car's headlights veered up Liberty Ave and I moved away from the sudden glare that illuminated the trash can at the end of Elliot's driveway. A trash can stuffed with discarded belongings, waiting for the city collection that was still four days in the future.

Chapter Nineteen

MOM FAINTED AT THE DOCTOR'S OFFICE, I MEAN *FAINTED*.
To get my cast off I wore this new girly shirt
instead of a sloppy weekend T-shirt or dress-code
collared school shirt. Mom was excited too, but she
didn't look too good when Dr. Andrews took out the
pin. I'd been dying to see what it looked like since
it'd been covered up all those weeks. It was silver
metal thick as a paper clip, shaped like an L, and
punched right into my skin through the gauze that
had gotten all crummy and crushed. It was scabby
and gross where it stuck in my arm and Dr. Andrews
had to pick off the crust, which was more like nose
stuff than blood stuff.

He gave me the pin for a souvenir, then called in
a nurse to cut off the rest of the gauze since it was
glued to my wrinkled-up arm. She started snipping
at my wrist and worked right up to my elbow and

past the pin place, and then she accidentally sliced a perfect V in my upper arm and the skin gapped open like it was too surprised to start bleeding and you could see exactly how thick the epidermis is, like I learned at school, and then it started gushing blood and I started crying and Mom fell on the floor. *Cooled out* is what Whit would say. Would have said, I mean.

For a minute—while one nurse was putting *another* bandage on me and saying she was sorry all over the place, and another nurse was picking Mom up off the floor—I thought Mom might be pregnant or something. But no way, she's too old. To torture me Whit used to tell me, I was an accident, but nobody has to have a baby if they don't want one.

I'll have a scar now, like *Me, Eloise*. Wait, no, it's Madeline who has the scar.

"Me and Bett are taking some big trash bags down to the park and clean up so maybe a newspaper man will come by and take our picture," I told Mom on the way home. "Like Whit with the hockey stick and you and Elliot with the snowmen."

"Why don't you ask Bett to spend the night? You've spent lots of nights with her but she's never stayed at our house."

"Bett doesn't spend the night out."

"What?"

"She's afraid to."

Mom laughed hard. "I can't believe it."

Today is a Hoot day. Sometimes Mom thinks Bett is a Hoot and sometimes she thinks she's a Pain. "Pia," Whit would say, for pain-in-the-ass. "Kia," he called know-it-alls, like Anne. Mom would croak if she knew Whit talked to me like that.

"Worldly Bett, afraid to spend the night out?" Mom said, still laughing.

I don't know what "worldly" means, but I don't hold it against Bett that she can't do sleepovers. Since Dad moved out I like a light on in the hall at night while we're asleep so that the robber who broke our window will know someone's home. Then I think, but if I leave the light on in the hall, the robber will think we've left the light on so he'll just *think* we're home, so he can break in again. And then I think that if I leave the light on in the hall it'll just light the way, make it easier for him. But if I don't leave it on he'll think we're not home.

Well, it's complicated, and I get up a lot at night to check on things. But it's not like pulling on my arm hairs and rubbing the skin raw, which I stopped doing, like, *ages* ago. Even though I still miss Whit, the sight of a car's taillights disappearing down Liberty Ave doesn't make me sad anymore. I'm older now, going into seventh grade after the summer, and now that I'm older, what Mom told me the Dead Snowman afternoon makes total sense. *After* she'd yelled at me for saying "Dead snowman" over and over whenever we passed scarves and hats and stuff lying on the ground.

"It's a little like cremation," she said.

"How?"

"The snowmen are gone but the gloves are still there."

"So?"

"When you take your hand out of a glove, it's still shaped like your hand. The fingers curl up and the palm is poochy. But your hand has gone on doing other things. It doesn't need the glove to protect it anymore. Your hand is like a soul. It's gone on living somewhere else, and the body is just a thing that warmed it or kept it safe and dry. See what I mean?"

Well. That made sense. But how do they attach the wings?

A squirrel sat up on the side of the road, debating whether to run in front of the car.

"Squirrels have a death wish," Whit used to say. "They only run across the street when they see a car coming."

I used to scream when squirrels ran in front of us. "Never dodge an animal," Whit told me, "because you might hit something else. A mailbox, maybe even a person."

So now I told Mom, "Don't brake for that squirrel."

"Besides," Whit had told me, "who cares if you run over a squirrel? It's basically just a *rat*." Elliot had said the exact thing forever ago, last fall.

But just the same, I didn't want Mom to run over it. Whit said squirrels were rats just to torture me, the same way he used to tell me I was an accident baby, or say he wanted to play dolls with me. "Whit used to pretend like he was a daddy coming home from work to play with the baby and he'd throw my doll Junie up in the air and let her drop, splat, and laugh," I told Mom now.

She looked away from the road at me. I know I said something out of the blue, but I figure it's my job to remember stuff about Whit for Mom. "Remember how Whit said there was a trash can boogie man and a tool shed boogie man and an attic boogie man and an upstairs boogie man?" I know it sounds dumb, but if you had a brother who died you wouldn't think so.

"Only because it was dark," Mom said. "And you leave a light on now, remember?"

What I remembered was Elliot's joke the first day I met him. *Know how to make a tissue dance? You put a little boogie in it.* I'd like to talk about Elliot, too, but he's gone. The bank has, like, taken over his house and he had to move out.

"Evicted," Bett said. She watches a lot of Court TV.

"Was not," I said. "He moved. He can work wherever there's trees."

"Hunh," Bett said. "Guess what. My mother went to this disco party and there was a black light and her two front teeth are fake and so it looked like she had no teeth! Let's do a Shania Twain karaoke."

Mom and I drove under the telephone wires that stayed up even during the wind storm, and the shoes were still dangling by their laces—four of them now instead of two. "I wonder what those shoes are doing up there," Mom said. "Some teenager testing their pitching arm, I guess. Some *barefoot* teenager."

"They mean 'I've been here.'"

"Oh, really," Mom said, kinda smirky.

"Elliot told me so. The high-tops are his. We threw them up there together the night we went skitching."

She slowed down. The car, I mean, and the way she nodded, and even breathed. "I'm so glad Elliot was your friend, Ebie."

"We were going to do this phonetic secret language thing together. Whatever you write is spelled just like the word sounds. S-K-E-W-L for school and A-P-L for apple. So his name would be spelled E-Y-E-T."

"Maybe I can do the secret language with you."

I didn't say so to her, but why would I want to write notes to someone I see every day?

We were coming up Liberty Ave now. There's a big mansion with room for three cars but no yard going up on the corner, and I hear they have six kids.

Six! I wouldn't babysit for six kids, not for money. But we're moving anyway, to a new neighborhood that has all these historic rules that mean you can't add on to your house or paint it pink or anything. Mom says I can help pick out the house. "Elliot didn't stay for my piano recital. Even though I couldn't be *in* the recital because of my cast."

Mom pulled down the visor, but there wasn't any sun in her eyes. "No."

"He just vanished, like Meany Matheny did."

Mom shook her head. "No, not like that."

"Mary Poppins, then. Mary Poppins stayed until the wind changed, and our wind changed with the storm."

"Oh, Ebie."

"And you're like Sleeping Beauty."

"What do you mean?"

"Elliot cut through all the briars with his saws and made you wake up."

"He—" She put her hand to her forehead. "Hand me my sunglasses, would you?"

Normally she never lets anyone dig around in her pocketbook. "Do you love Elliot? Did you, I mean?"

She thought a pretty long time, but she was driving, so it's hard to tell if she was thinking about watching out for the other guy like she used to tell Whit, or whether she was thinking about my question.

"I did love him, yes," she finally said. "But I also

love you, and trees, and Darrell, and old glass beads, and watermelon and—"

"And Dad?" It wasn't a fair question. I said a long time ago that you can tell right off the bat what Mom loves and doesn't love.

"I loved Dad, too. But now I . . . like him. And you need to love someone to be married to them."

It was time to make her remember again. "Remember when Whit asked me if I was in the retardundo?" This made her smile. I knew it would.

We were almost home. I got ready to say, "Mom, the pothole is filled," like I always do even though she always forgets and swerves around it, which is just as dangerous as dodging a squirrel. But before I could even say it, this time she drove right over the pothole. The pothole that isn't there anymore anyway. The street people filled it in.

"Now that you have your arm back, will you play something for me before you go to the park with Bett?" Mom asked.

My arm didn't look as skinny and white as I hoped it would, like a mummy's. "Sure. What do you want to hear?" I wiggled my fingers and listed all the ones she liked. "'One Hand, One Heart,' 'Moon River,' 'Pachelbel Canon,' 'Beauty and the Beast,' 'Somewhere Over the Rainbow'—"

"Whatever you want," Mom interrupted me. "You pick."

Chapter Twenty

THERE'S A LONG-RUNNING COLUMN TITLED "CAN THIS
Marriage Be Saved?" in one of the women's magazines. It's a transcription of a session between a husband and a wife and a marriage therapist in which
problems and issues are discussed and dissected. At
the article's conclusion, the counselor passes professional judgment on the likelihood of the relationship's continuing, and advises the readers and the
couple how best to resolve their differences. In one
month's article the therapist concluded that no, this
marriage could not be saved. The resulting flood of
readership mail was so universally dismayed and neg-
ative that the editors did everything but retract the
piece, and for fear of losing subscribers, never again
risked predicting an unhappy marital outcome.

I love the irony of this. We want to know the
ending, but only if the ending is happy. I suspect the

underlying reason is that a reader often recognizes herself and her own marriage in the column's depiction, and needs reassurance that she, and her marriage, will live happily ever after.

But when a child dies, the dream of a whole and happy family dies, too. You're supposed to go on living when the reason to live has vanished.

Russ and I always took two cars to church because I wanted to get there early and enjoy the quiet before the service. Sometimes Russ's car would loom up behind mine at an interminable stoplight on the way to church, and Ebie and I would wave in the rearview mirror at Russ and Whit behind us as we waited together. On Sunday mornings the green light is timed to last mere seconds, and Russ would race across six lanes beneath a yellow light. Safe on the other side, I'd think the unthinkable, imagine the might-have-been, nearly hear the squeal of brakes, the crash. The accident.

"There's no such thing as an accident. Any psychiatrist will tell you that," Anne once casually pronounced. As if Whit's death wasn't an accident. As if Teddy Strickland's death wasn't an accident. Was my sleeping with Elliot Hatcher an accident?

Yes.

No.

"It's because of Elliot, isn't it?" Ebie asked me as I sliced bananas for her sandwich. "You and Dad."

"No," I told her.

People need reasons. They need to know if it was *mutual*. They need to take a *side*. They need an injured party. They need tangibles, not abstractions. Whether it happened because of the husband's wet towels and dirty socks in the bathroom or the wife's unwashed dishes and unshaved legs. That someone was chronically late or chronically dull or didn't make enough money or wasn't a good mother. That someone was dishonest or that someone was unfaithful, and aren't they ultimately both the same?

"There's not one good reason to let Darrell go," I'd said to Russ before I knew the entire truth. Before I slept with Elliot.

"It's the cumulative effect," Russ said. "We have different interests now, and want the company to go in different directions."

Cumulative effects. Different directions. Reasons enough for the end of a marriage as well. The statistics for a marriage's survival when a child dies are dismal, greater than any other adversity. Like the roots of a black walnut tree, loss secretes a toxic substance so that nothing can grow. Some tragedies unite, others divide.

What reasons would Elliot give? "It died of natural causes," he said of trees, and many do: drought, age, disease.

"It's not because of Elliot," I told Ebie. "Daddy

and I ... we didn't take care of each other. And we disappointed each other." Even eleven-year-olds need reasons. "You'll see Daddy as much as you want to."

"How about you?"

I shook potato chips onto her lunch plate. Russ and I had parted without melodrama or melodramatic pain. We had worn out our pain. It had leached from us, tired and stretched like elastic in an old bathing suit. "Right now neither of us much wants to see the other."

"But *will* you?"

When my daughter lay limp and injured on the snowy street I'd mentally telegraphed her: *You are all I have left.* Even then, I knew. Even then I hadn't included Russ in my *all*.

"Maybe someday," I told Ebie.

But no. Too much water under too many burned bridges.

One morning last week I drove past our old house. The boxwoods are full again, with no sign of snow damage. Their leafy branches were draped with dozens of cobwebs like fairy hammocks, silvery with dew. The ivy has begun to come back, too, like a patch of grass that has been there all along and suddenly appears beneath melting snow. Whit will not come back. Nor will Elliot, or Teddy, or I.

The split-rail fence where Elliot and I had perched, drained yet triumphant, after conquering the ivy, had fallen down while I wasn't watching, so the boundary between our houses has disappeared. While I wasn't watching, Elliot moved in. While I wasn't watching, he moved out. While I wasn't watching, my marriage ended. While I wasn't watching, Whit died.

Was Elliot-the-man an invention of desire, or was Elliot-the-boy a substitute for a son? Had he given me back my son, or given me back myself? All and none. What was it, then, between us? Infidelity driven by friendship, desire, and sorrow. I sought consolation in him; he sought comfort in me.

"He didn't even say good-bye," Ebie said. Non sequitur or not, I knew who she was talking about.

He did to me, after a fashion. When you make love with someone you forever have a piece of them and they forever have a piece of you, just as I'd told Whit. Sometimes sex isn't an act of loving but of lamenting.

"Here's your lunch," I said. "It's almost time for camp." This summer Ebie's taking afternoon lessons in piano and theater and filmmaking at the Cultural Arts Center.

At five o'clock I park and wait for her and watch a young boy making his way across the lot toward his mother's car. The gait, the body shape, the backpack on his shoulders, the curling hair render him instantly to me—Whit—and I clutch the steering wheel, breathless. There will always be minefields, always be reminders, always be pain. Grief is the price we pay for attachments. "I want my windows both open *and* closed," I'd told Elliot when I stood at his, wrapped in his sheet. "I want to listen to birds and children and feel the breezes. But I don't want to hear leaf blowers or sirens, and bugs coming in the house, and the sills getting grimy with pollen."

Elliot's response was simple: "You can't have it both ways."

"You use one tree to kill its brother," I'd said to Elliot the afternoon I watched him work. "The tree is an unwitting accomplice."

"If you want to look at it like that," he'd said. I used Elliot to recover from Whit, and then he used me, too. Like trees, we were both victims and villains. And then he'd quoted Willa Cather: "'I like trees because they seem more resigned to the way they have to live than other things.'"

I think of the teenagers in the decorated Homecoming car that same glorious afternoon; their sheer happiness and absolute unawareness of any time beyond This Very Minute, beyond a perfect song suddenly playing on the radio. It seems to me those moments occur most often in adolescence. Before then you aren't aware enough, don't know enough, to recognize pure joy. Moments of perfect glee and incandescent happiness are spontaneous. They can't be planned, can't be orchestrated. Yet for the rest of our lives we unconsciously try to replicate or replace or rediscover them, to attain again that surge of uncomplicated, absolute joy. Ripping ivy is one way, or building snowmen, or rolling a house.

He couldn't give me back my son, but he gave me back my joy.

The house sold in October. Russ mailed me a check, my portion of the proceeds, and in the same envelope enclosed a letter addressed to Ebie Lucas, on Liberty Avenue.

"For me?" Ebie said excitedly. "I never get mail! From who?"

"I don't know," I said. There wasn't a return address, only a postmark stamped Seattle.

She ripped into it, a Halloween card. "I found the scariest sight I could to send you on Halloween," the black printing proclaimed on the front. She opened it to a wavery piece of mirror glued inside, and a recording of a realistically bloodcurdling scream. *Eeeeeeeeeekkkk!*

I laughed at the sound effect. "Maybe we should use that as our answering machine message."

"It's from Elliot," Ebie said, a wide grin on her face.

"How do you know, did he sign it?" I asked,